Gatherings Volume 14

The En'owkin Journal of First North American Peoples

En'owkin Reunion

Fall 2003

Edited by
Karen W. Olson

Theytus Books Ltd.
Penticton, BC

Gatherings
The En'owkin Journal of First North American Peoples Volume 14
2003

National Library of Canada Cataloguing in Publication Data

Main entry under title:

Gatherings

Annual.
ISSN 1180-0666
ISBN 1-894778-12 X (v. 14)

1. Canadian literature (English)--Indian authors--Periodicals.* 2. Canadian literature (English)--Periodicals.* 3. American literature--Indian authors-- Periodicals. 4. American literature--Periodicals. I. En'owkin International School of Writing. II. En'owkin Centre.
PS8235.I6G35 C810.8'0897 CS91-031483-7
PR9194.5.I5G35

Editorial Committee: Jeannette Armstrong and Karen W. Olson
Cover Painting: "Return to the River" by Lee Claremont
Layout and Design: Leanne Flett Kruger
Proofing: Regina 'Chick' Gabriel and Tara Jack

Please send submissions and letters to
Gatherings,
En'owkin Centre, R.R.#2, Site 50, Comp. 8
Penticton, BC
V2A 6J7, Canada.
Previously published works are not considered.

The publisher acknowledges the support of the Canada Council for the Arts, the Department of Canadian Heritage and the British Columbia Arts Council in publication of this book.

Gatherings
Volume 14

En'owkin Reunion

Table of Contents

First Words

Section 1 – Splashes From Paddle's Tip

Section 2 –
The Grandmothers are Dancing in my Hair

Section 3 – Family Gathering

Section 4 – Rushing Water

Table of Contents

Section 5 – Dramatic Writings

Section 6 – Images

Artists:

First Words

Editor's Note:

The En'owkin Centre is one of Canada's foremost Indigenous Arts schools. Nestled in BC's Okanagan valley, the school offers a Certificate in Foundations in Indigenous Fine Arts through the University of Victoria, Okanagan Adult Language Immersion, College Readiness, Indigenous Political Development and Leadership, and the National Aboriginal Professional Artist Training program. Since 1985, when post-secondary classes began, over 500 students have come to learn and share knowledge here. *Gatherings* was first published in 1990 and remains an important element in First Nation literary arts. This edition is a reunion issue featuring those students, instructors and mentors who have graced our circle of learning with their creative talents.

The En'owkin Centre holds a singular place in my heart for it was here, from 1997 to 1999, that I found the trail that led to a pool of creativity that lay resting and waiting within. As a former journalist in mass media I had been trained to repress creative urges and remain focused on the who, what, where, when, why and how of a story… dry reportage. Then the pool began to overflow, it began to leak, and droplets of creative writing emerged. Today, I cannot imagine a day without writing something creative, even if it is only a silly note to my daughter. Therefore, when asked to be the editor of a *Gatherings* that would reunite the En'owkin family, I felt truly honored.

Former and present instructors, mentors and students of the En'owkin Centre (our extended family) were invited to come together on the pages of a special issue of Gatherings. Although our family has taken paths which led them to far places, we found many. Richard Van Camp, Joy Kogawa, Armand Garnet Ruffo, Drew Hayden Taylor, William George, Rasunah Marsden, Krystal Cook and others sent writing which reflects upon their time in the Okanagan valley or allows a glance into their present state of creative being. To our family members we were unable to find, we miss you and hope to hear from you soon.

When a family comes together there is joy and laughter, tears and sorrow, stories and tall tales, hugs and kisses, and happiness in making their circle strong once more. You, dear Reader, will find all that and much more in these pages. Enjoy.

Gathering Berries and Words

The idea of creating an annual journal/collection of new writing by First North American Peoples came out of a discussion between Lee Maracle, Mini Freeman, Joy Harjo, Margo Kane and myself in the initial formation of the En'owkin School of Writing as a program during the Moon of Ripe Siya' (Saskatoon Berries) June 1990. I remember that day. Joy, Mini, Margo and I gathered at En'owkin Centre's Brunswick Street site to talk about the school and how the perspectives and materials in the writing courses must be founded on the most current writing. During the discussion, my mother and older sisters arrived to let me know they were on their way to pick berries, and asked, "Why can't you continue the discussion while you are picking berries?" Margo, Joy and Mini agreed immediately and we set out in a car following them, leaving a note for Lee to catch up when she arrived. Lee did catch up later and we had a great time picking berries and talk, talk, talking about the Writing School program. There is something wonderful and juicy about picking berries with women which speaks of fertility and voluptuous abundance and the warm sun and survival and renewal; it spoke to us of the rightness of what we were trying to put in place. I think we were listened to that day and were given the permission and the help to sustain this work.

The idea of creating a yearly journal of new writing flowed out of that discussion, and continued over the next three days of visiting at the En'owkin Centre and at my house for a family gathering. Someone said, "We need a gathering of writing, every year." Someone else said, "Just like the old time gatherings every year." Someone else said, "Yeah, the campout ones in which people who live a long ways apart, exchange stories and get caught up on anything new." Someone else added, "We could call it gatherings or something like that." I admit that I can't remember who said exactly what and when and that is probably good because the whole idea is wrapped up in that wonderful time with those great women. It belongs to all of us. It is our *Gatherings*.

The first volume, which Lee and I edited, came out in the fall of 1990 after a memorable hot summer at OKA. We are indebted to the Canada Council of the Arts for supporting the publication of the first volumes. Since then, I have looked forward each year to its publication with such anticipation. When I read it, it is like sitting at a gathering of our people from across Turtle Island. I am looking forward to this reunion volume. It feeds and nurtures the hunger I have to hear the stories of our people. I hope we will continue to have *Gatherings* for a long time to come.

Jeannette C. Armstrong.
Chokecherry Moon, 2003

Gatherings

Over time, most literary magazines last less than two years. One of the possible reasons for their demise might well be that they are either theme magazines or, are supported by government or private donor finances. When war has ended perhaps there is no need for a magazine devoted to war or whatever other theme. Yet, if a writer should look into the small press publishers and literary magazines they would find countless magazines devoted to themes.

The great beauty and wonder concerning *Gatherings* is the quality of the work which has been the cause for its longevity, even though it is basically a theme magazine. Few publications dealing with Native American (First Person) themes seem to survive time. Difficult to understand why, as Native Peoples are definitely here to stay and continue to make an enormous contribution to the present and the future. *Gatherings* has done and continues to do exactly that – contribute. It is known for publishing over many active years a very large number of recognized writers who hail from both Canada and the United States (there is no Creative border). Beth Cuthand, Richard Greene, Raven Hail, Jeannette Armstrong, Lee Maracle, Drew Taylor, Lorne Simon, Joy Harjo, Peter Blue Cloud, Joseph Bruchac and Kimberly Blazer have been published in the pages, along with many other known and emerging writers.

It is an established fact that the En'owkin Centre was the dream miracle of Jeannette Armstrong, a thoroughly committed teacher and writer of no small international importance. With the support of her people and the aid of Don Fiddler, this incredible vision has given a strong foundation to many Native writers who would turn to the Centre for clarity, confidence, method, and sustenance which all Creative people need to survive and produce whatever arts may come from their rich imagination.

In the Monashee range of the eastern Cascades slopes rising from the shores of Skaha Lake's slate grey waters where coyote winds howl across the Okanagan valley, the En'owkin Centre was first established to offer any and all Native peoples a place to invent a new perspective on creativity, whatever their age or gender. A validation of life, a dream miracle, a confirmation through dedication and importance was given along with whatever certificate granted at the end of study.

Out of this original miracle rose another miracle. Theytus Books Ltd. brought forth a literary magazine of substantial, beautiful and meaningful Native writing. *Gatherings*, under the editorship of Greg Young-Ing, Florene Belmore (a former student at the Centre), Kateri Akiwenzie-Damm, Jeannette Armstrong and others, is a truly impressive publication which has crossed the known world with its beauty and import. From 1990 to present day, this magazine continues to survive literary winds and produces some of the most important literature in the known world. We honor the editors and their visions. We wish it continued success and positive support to emerging writers and students of Native literatures.

The original vision holds, deepens, widens and circles the lives and imaginations of many Native peoples who may well have been ignored by other quarters of the literary world. Native literature is nothing new. Storytelling, poems and song have flourished since the beginning. We graciously thank the dreamers for their dreams.

Maurice Kenny
In the Adirondack Mountains

Section 1

Splashes From Paddle's Tip

Canoe

go
blood drop   rain drop   tear drop

hhoo   hhoo   hhoo
Cedar stands strong and honorable
for hundreds and thousands of years
standing deep-rooted to earth
and during those years
Cedar dreams of becoming canoe
dreaming a vessel
carved from wood and spirit
heart and song and breath
Cedar dreams a vessel
paddling through generations
paddling through nations
hhoo   hhoo   hhoo

go
tear drop   blood drop   rain drop

hhoo   hhoo   hhoo
paddles pump in unison
ocean salt spray
splashes from paddle's tip
hhoo   hhoo   hhoo
community togetherness
hhoo   hhoo   hhoo
survival
fishing hunting gathering
hhoo   hhoo   hhoo

go
blood drop   tear drop   rain drop

hhoo   hhoo   hhoo
breath   exhale and breath again

and in between those breaths
Cedar dreams of becoming great canoe
to the ocean to the ocean
Cedar dreams of being war canoe
to the ocean to the ocean
canoe journeys out to the ocean
with majesty and respect
Cedar canoe
hhoo   hhoo   hhoo

go
rain drop   blood drop   tear drop

hhoo   hhoo   hhoo
as the Indian river
flows into the burrard inlet
flowing out to the ocean
my grandfather and grandfathers
paddled in canoes
instead of cedar carved canoe I have a pen
hhoo   hhoo   hhoo

go
tear drop   rain drop   blood drop in my canoe

my canoe – asking praying knowing I am my canoe
cedar my canoe is my pen
the paddle words I share again
HHOO   HHOO   HHOO

i am from….

i
am
from
northern lights
sparkling stars of midnight
dark
eyes filled with insight
i am from bright moons
shifting moons
i am from childhood kites trying to
touch the blue sky drifting at noon
when only grey clouds
feel fields of wishful dandelions

i am from scripted lines of star filled
happy days…friends…star wars…another world
i am from pablo neruda, pablo picasso,
pavlov's dog and pablum
i am from prosthetic memories and
protected memories

i am from desires, wants, needs
i am from twisting tiger lilies and weeds
twisting tongues and hearts planting seeds

i am from the land of logos, egos and
diluted goals
and a dream house made of legos
i am from barbie dolls
jam packed malls and
shopping centers

i am from the middle
in the middle
of vast skies and sky scrapers

i am from, in a sense,
innocence
and i am from, in a sense,
experience

Kissing Day

Well I finally figured'er out.
When I was a boy growing up in Fort Smith
I remember the parties my parents threw.

New Year's Eve
Lots of fun
Stayed up late, boy, watchin' everything.
Come midnight
all the adults run around kissin' everyone.
Lights out!
Women kissin' men!
Men kissin' women!
Some took off to the bathroom or basement.
Took a long time gettin'er done!

I read today from a Cree Elder that they used to call Christmas and New Year's
"Kissing Day"
because that's what they did.

I guess the Crees learned my folks and they wanted to share it, eh?
There's lots of Crees in Smith
but no Crees at our parties…

So I started thinking that if you've been married for ten years,
I bet you'd get curious about someone else,
how they'd kiss maybe
or move against you maybe.

(What would you do if you had five minutes alone with someone again?)

So I guess you got to make it count on Kissing Day.
Make you feel good for a whole year
'til next time.

And maybe that's why I get kicked out of all these New Year's
parties now.
I'm runnin' 'round kissin' women, eh?
Feels good but I catch heck in the truck all the way home.

That's the way she goes, I guess…

So God bless the Crees and God bless my folks and good golly God bless my ol' lady for putting up with me – even though she's runnin' 'round kissin' people too!

Remembering Lorne Simon

October 1994

The tragic news of Lorne Simon's untimely death shocked and deeply saddened all who had come to love him and his writing. He was loved by and influenced many native writers who were in personal contact with him. He kept in constant touch with many fellow native writers by letter. Instead of ordinary letters, Lorne wrote poems and stories to fellow writers. It was always with wonderful anticipation that I opened his letters of ten or more pages. I knew Lorne as a deeply contemplative young artist whose writing, though he had just begun to publish, had reached a maturity which promised a future as one of Canada's most significant native writers. His contribution to us has had a deep impact.

His own words, from a letter I received shortly before his death, gave insight into an important vision which he had. He said, "You wrote in one of the cards that you recently spoke to the public on the excitement you felt about the work native writers will be doing in the future in reclaiming and revitalizing their past and their cultural heritage. I do feel that I am part of this exciting development. While currently there are hardly any Mi'kmaq writers who are vigorously taking part in this effort, I am sure that I will be setting an example and that others will follow. This, what I am doing, is a ripple emanating from a pearl thrown into the pool of talent. Keep throwing pearls into the pool, for they are not wasted."

Lorne Simon will be missed and there will always be a void which only his talent would have filled. His words, his time here, will not be wasted. A movement which can only widen into greater circles has begun. Those to follow, to add their pearls, will have his words and his deepest wish, to reclaim and revitalize what is native, to guide them to the pool.

Night

En'owkin class assignment 1991

Nothing, it seemed to him now, had ever gone right. He stood, breathing spasmodically, on the trail that entered into the woods behind his parent's house. It was night. The stars sent the liquid luster reflection of Trenton's lights on the still bay. The clouds hung like thin veils one could brush aside to afford an unobstructed view of the fast rising moon. A breeze whispered through the poplars carrying the scent of sweetgrass. In his right fist, Gordon clenched his father's hunting knife.

His dark eyes turned inward where a fire burned. Of the nineteen years of his life, Gordon, bitterly and shamefully, could only count his earliest years as a time he had known happiness.

"Those years. Were they real? They are like those dark clouds – distant, illusory. I can't even say with certainty I was happy once!"

No echo answered this outburst, only the rustle of the leaves and the life of Trenton could be heard. Gordon's bitterness could find no words, he rejected them with contempt. His eyes clenched shut. A groan crawled out from the pit of his stomach.

"Oh, soul, be free!" He wanted to cry out but felt an overpowering disgust for words. Words argued until they bogged him down with only one thing that, in the end, was certain – uncertainty. One action became as useless as another. More than ever, Gordon longed to leap beyond language into the silent omniscience that he imagined cosmic awareness to be. His thoughts would not quit; they moved deliberately, shifted randomly like the sudden gusts that shook the leaves.

He blamed his older brother Phillip for having cut short his happy years. Gordon had been his parent's favorite. When Gordon turned six, Phillip began to beat on him. The beatings desecrated his spirit. Shame followed every beating. Out of pride and so as not to reveal his shame, he endured years of beatings and never once told on his brother. By the time he turned eleven he felt that everything good in him had been violated and that he was guilty for it. Had he really deserved to be loved by his parents so much more? When he turned fifteen and towered over his brother, he did not avenge himself.

With a sharp intake of air, his mouth and lungs detected the mysterious thickening presence of dew. Had he looked to the left he would have seen fine silvery threads endlessly weaving a trail through the darkening woods, the filament drooping like strings of pearls under the gathering crystals of dew. He would have seen the familiar and enchanting dome of light pulsing several miles to the north indicating the seaside Acadian village of St-Antoine. Had he glanced up he would not have waited long to witness the blazing descent of a falling star.

Gordon clung to the picture of his lost innocence. He wanted to savor the bitterness before turning his thoughts to a more torturous matter. He recalled the simple faith he once had in God. There was a belief in the village of Trenton that if you saved a person from certain death the rescuer was assured a place in Paradise. Gordon saw himself as a boy, a small solitary figure walking along the shore looking out at the waters for some poor drowning swimmer to save. The picture struck him as poignant at first. He used to feel the certainty of faith, everything around him used to be vital. He used to be naïve. "Naïve," spat from his lips and his eyes flooded. The past was nothing but pathetic sentimentality.

His watery eyes looked on as Venus pulsed and grew. He thought of Christ in the garden and saw not the savior, but a sad and broken man. The knife would be Gordon's bitter cup.

Laughter and the incessant barking of dogs became muffled in the solemn dignity of the forest. "The weekend – and everyone my age is having fun," he thought. The shrill and exaggerated laugh of a young girl echoed through the village followed by the shouts of bold carousers. Cars roared. Tires squealed. Suddenly, the thing that was tearing most at Gordon's heart leapt to the fore of his thoughts.

"I loved you, Daria!" he screamed. "You goddamn bitch, I loved you!"

He fell silent, jaw slack, and for a long moment Daria's face, her body, her dazzling smile, her laughter and her mischievous eyes filled his mind and blinded him to the world. Such beauty! He regretted his harshness and was ashamed of what he had just called her. He cursed his morbid and sensitive nature which seemed forever at odds with the frivolous nature of the world. His anger grew.

"You told me you loved me," he cried. "But you don't know what love is or what a treasure you are. You throw yourself at any man who will buy you a good time. Is it because you want to show me that you can have any man?" Silence. "No. You will never see me jealous. Why should I hate another man when you have encouraged him? It is you I must banish from my heart. You!"

But Gordon knew he could not do it. He had no resolve. All he could see before him was terrifying loneliness, a vast and empty cavern that swallowed him and his future. It would always be this way. Forever apart, alone in his pain and humiliation. Others had some kind of marginal happiness – a family and domestic contentment.

Why does eternity torment me?

Love meant to hold exclusively and to be held exclusively for all time and beyond death. Gordon knew this union which he hungered for was ideal, but his passionate soul could not settle for anything less. *Born alone to die alone*. The thought flashed through his mind.

"Why?"

He began to yell as though a javelin from the cold distances of space had pierced him.

"Answer me!" he yelled."If you exist, God, show me a sign! Let that be Your answer! I shall forever be soothed! I shall be Your most devout servant! Just show me a sign! Tell me that there is more than this bleak night! A sign, God, a sign! No one, I promise You, will love You more than I! No one will worship You more or show greater reverence than I if You will only show me a sign! Dear God, if You exist…"

His ranting became incoherent. He remained on his feet, a small part of him fully expecting a sign. In the quiet that followed the breeze moaned like a phantom mourning for all transience.

"Damn you," Gordon yelled. "If You don't exist than neither does the Beast! Still, if he appeared I would kiss his feet and be a slave forever. Just tell me Satan, that there is more than this night. Just tell me that the soul lives forever!"

The stars remained mute like a host of friends smiling and dumb in their conspiracy. A pale green moon cleared the clouds and sent florescent light rushing over the earth to penetrate the forest. A bat flew overhead, oblivious to everything below, intent only on reaching its destination. The breeze moved searchingly through the forest, transforming itself from an indefinable ether form to an almost solid hulk that could shake the trees. A frightened little creature scurried over the twigs and dead leaves.

“What is there to live for then?” Gordon asked with his head bowed low.

In an instant, he was strangely alert, his eyes open wide and his head cocked. He gasped, “And Lord, nothing… nothing to die for!” He choked for a moment on his sobs before they burst out like the cough of a sick beast. His fingers turned icy. The knife dropped. He wept.

wild gorgeous beast

the perch were
shoving and swimming
shoving
and swimming
they were so many so small
blurred
bound by the swim
the jostle of mystical memory

dad took me and Beth down
to Amisk River to
watch the men brown with summer
scoop their meals out with the nets
slotted spoons that left only the golden cream

dad wandered off to the trucks
parked on the high dirt road to
bullshit and laugh with the men
they loaded
red and white coolers of perch into their pickups
they shed green rubber waders
dried wet arms hands

i plopped down on the sandy embankment
watched Beth
wade into the green river
measured steps the river metered out
small short steps to her final note by the rocks

and the fish thought she was one of the still smooth
stones in the stream
letting the water rush by her
the rapid excited buzz of her pulse slowed
chilled by the icy flow

as she slowly bent down
she was the dancing shadow of a swaying poplar tree
the sun was kind
winking her dark then light dark then light
the fish were hypnotized

her hands slipped
under a cold slimy belly
she flipped a fish onto the
sandy shore to slap and jump at my feet

Nature's camouflage tricked my eyes too
one blink
and the wild gorgeous beast before me
wore my sister's black rubber boots.

Reunion

Pigs were squealing, trying to dig deeper into the mud to escape the afternoon heat. My oldest brother Henry told me that pigs can't sweat. That's why it's dumb to say, "*Sweat like a pig*". I shivered and scratched at an imaginary bug crawling under my yellow t-shirt and up my back. Pigs are gross, they will eat anything. That's why feeding them is not part of my chores. Jack says that having my hands near the trough would be enough for them to start chewing them off. Ugh!

Henry says little Indian girls with green eyes are the yummiest and that's why I get bit more, even from the mosquitoes. Teenagers are so dumb.

I had fed and watered the chickens and now they dotted the lush green of the yard. They seemed to scratch around at nothing, probably looking for little bugs. I ran towards one throwing my hands in the air and making scary gobble-de-gook noises. I laughed and shook my head. She didn't try to run very far, just a loud squawk and a jump.

Oops! I forgot I was trying to be quiet. I took the softest steps I could across the yard; my brown ponytail bounced against the middle of my back like the finger of a friend egging me on. It was the middle of July and my cousins were coming to visit for the reserve's pow-wow; I wanted to fix up my room. I skipped up the porch stairs, took off my black rubber boots and inched the screen door open. Safe. Mom and Jen weren't in the kitchen. I had to be careful because lately, conversations at our dinner table became a debate on how many chores an eight year old was capable of doing. Jen, my older sister, believes in child labour.

I slid down the hallway in my white socks, the slight breeze brushed back my bangs. I jumped to hug the wall as I passed my parent's room. Mom on her bed with a small box in her hands. My room is next door and I tiptoed to it. Carefully turning the doorknob closed, I let out a breath.

"Mom. Mom!"

It was Jen yelling. Jen is a teenager, and Mom really likes to go shopping with her. Jen says that it is unfair that she has brown eyes and that I'm pretty 'cause I don't even care what I look like. One time, she offered to paint my nails. I had so much dirt under my fingernails she called me a heathen. I asked Dad what that meant and he said Jen was jealous of me because I'm a real farm girl.

"Could you please help me?"

Jen was right outside my parent's room but yelling as if she was outside in the garden. "I need you to tell me which one looks good. Come on."

I lean against my door, listening to their footsteps going down the hall. That was too close for me; I should go back outside. I started down the hall but froze when I heard the bathroom door open. I ducked into Mom and Dad's room.

We weren't allowed in my parent's room but I felt safe as long as I heard the buzz of my Mom and Jen in the bathroom next door. The room always had a subtle bleach smell; it smelled fresh like their sheets, hot white and baked in the sun. Their bedroom was clean (not one piece of clothing on the floor) and cozy, the crazy quilt on the bed was a kaleidoscope of stories and colour. The little box still on the bed. The lid was flipped open and the brown paper lining was stained and frayed at the corners. Inside was a small wooden carving. I picked it up. It was a little girl with a bob haircut wearing a dress, smooth, except for the face. I rubbed my thumb over the sharp nose and chin.

Danger. The hive next door went quiet. The soft shuffle of Mom's slippers on the wooden hallway floor beat down the rumble of adrenalin in my ears. I dropped the carving back into the box, ran to the other side of the bed and dove under. I knew I would fit because last year my parents had attended a dance. Jen was babysitting me when we decided to dig out the two cardboard boxes under here. We expected to find treasure but only found neatly folded old clothes that stunk of mothballs.

I grabbed my mouth, willing myself to breathe normally. I stayed on my belly with the breath from my nose scattering the dust balls. The tile was hard and cold like a frozen winter pond against my legs. I wished I wasn't wearing shorts. I wished I had never come into this room. I shimmied over and positioned myself next to the boxes. I was like a huge chamois, picking up all the dust, dirt and loose hairs from the floor. I never ever thought it would be this dirty under here. I turned my head sideways and watched the blue moccasins step into the room.

Mom was bare legged. When she sat on the bed it gave a deep creak as though welcoming her back. I smelled the perfume of the apple lotion she rubbed on every morning and night. On her skin it smelled like apple rhubarb pie. In the reflection of the full-length mirror I could see Mom in her denim skirt and green plaid shirt. She picked up the carving. Suddenly she slumped onto the bed. I started to crawl out but the bed began to shake. So I curled into a ball and covered my head. As quickly as th shaking started, it stopped. I unfurled myself when I heard Mom speak.

"*Tansi.*"

I opened my eyes and blinked away the dust on my eyelashes.

"Ah, it's hard to get a moment to myself when the kids are home during the summer. Vicki is no problem to chase outside, I hardly see her until dinner. But Jen."

I rubbed my eyes. Who was my mom talking to? I watched her in the mirror. She looked toward the bottom of the bed, smiled and shook her head. I could see no legs. Maybe it was just Dad who jumped onto the bed, but he wasn't out in the field with my brothers Jack and Henry?

"Oh? Hmmm."

I wanted to hide behind the protective cover of the boxes but didn't want to move because I could see her green eyes narrow and squint into the mirror. She leaned forward, closer to the mirror, the carving in her hand. She sat back and looked to my side of the bed.

"It's so sweet. Ha. I never did such a thing." She giggled. "Oh yes, I do remember that time when you found us crawling between the bales. You gave me the worst spankin'. Bah, it wasn't because I was your favorite."

Then Mom stood and stretched. "Well, it might be funny to stay here all day, and see what kind of surprises I might find right under my nose, but I have to go to town today. And I want to have a coffee before I go."

She shuffled out of the room and went down the hallway. I dropped my head to the floor. I finally could get out of here. As I started to slide out, a pair of legs suddenly blocked me. The big brown boots were scuffed and well worn.

"Well, you gonna come outta there?" said a man's deep voice.

Caught. I was in trouble now. The legs moved over to give me room so I slid out and pulled myself up. I looked up at a very tall old man. He was skinny with hands as big as my brother Henry's. He wore blue jean overalls and a brown buttoned up shirt. He held a cap in his right hand that he switched to his left one and held out the empty hand to me. "Come on let's go see your mom."

I stared at him. His hand felt warm on mine. I was ashamed that my hand was cold. I wanted to tear it out of his grasp but his hands felt like my dad's hard hands. I could feel every ridge. His boots echoed on the wooden floor of the hallway. He paused slightly to look at the black and white pictures that were on the walls.

"Those are my ancestors," I said.

"Hmm. That so?" he chuckled and squeezed my hand.

I looked at a favorite picture of my *Kokom* on her wedding day. She looked really pretty and I liked to guess what color her sweater was when the picture was taken. As I stared at the picture, out of the corner of my eye I realized the man as tall as Henry and Jack. I peeked at him, quickly then back at the pictures on the wall.

He was looking at a picture of my great grandfather with his teenage children, Harry his oldest son, and his oldest daughter, Emma (my *Kokom*). My great grandfather was tall. Everyone said that's how Henry and Jack got their tallness. Because my Mom and Dad were short. In the picture Jonah, my great grandfather, was dressed in a dark suit although he looked sort of mean and he wasn't smiling at all.

I looked at the picture, looked at the man, looked at the picture, looked at the man. He looked down at me and I whipped my head low to stare at my feet. I licked my dry lips. My hands felt clammy, especially the one he held. So I tried to wriggle it out from his gentle hold.

"Wh-who are you?" I asked. He let go of my hand. I wiped them on my t-shirt, my favorite yellow one with Tweety Bird on it. He shifted from side to side. With a small smile that was kind of sad, his hand came up to rest on his lips. I took his free hand.

"This is me."

I pulled him to the bright school pictures of my brothers, sister and me, " I only got two school pictures up there." I led him toward the kitchen.

"Henry and Jack got lots up there, 'cause they're finished school. Jen gots lots too but she hates her pictures being on the wall." Mom was adding milk to her coffee and stirring it when we arrived.

"Oh-my-gosh."

The spoon fell inside the cup. She made the sign of the cross.

"Oh, Holy Christopher."

Small sobs escaped from her and her eyes welled up with tears. She ran over and hugged me.

"Can she see you?" she asked the old man. He nodded his head yes and patted me on the head.

"Oh-my-gosh."

A kernel of fear that popped into full-blown tears. I realized that Mom was not scared, she was crying for happiness.

"Vicki, this is my *Mooshom* Jonah. He is your great-grandfather."

My great-grandfather. I had never met my great-grandfather before. When my *Kokom* died, I was too little to remember her. At the time my *Mooshom* was living with a girlfriend in the city. When I looked up at Jonah, he smiled. He had green eyes – like Mom and me. I liked him. He laughed a deep rumbly laugh and leaned over to squeeze my shoulders in a hard hug.

"What's going on here?"

I didn't even hear Jen come upstairs from her room in the basement. She usually made so much noise that I imagined she was pulling a sack of mad turkeys up the stairs. Mom pulled herself straight and wiped her eyes.

"I love you girls. That's all." She walked over to Jen, hugged her and kissed her on the cheek.

"Ooo-kay." Jen patted my mom on the back and wriggled free from her hug.

I could barely contain myself and bit my tongue in excitement. Jen was going to be so surprised that our great-grandfather was here. I pointed to Jonah and smiled. Jen rolled her eyes and pushed past me.

" Whatever."

I latched onto her arm and she dragged me along for a few steps. "Get off, freak," She peeled my hands off and dropped me onto the beige linoleum floor.

She shook her head and turned to open the refrigerator door, "Oh great. Who keeps putting the pitcher back in here empty? Ugh."

Jen slammed the fridge door shut and stomped to the sink. When she turned on the tap I could feel her anger flowing like the water running from the tap.

"B-b-b-b-but Jen."

I was not even aware that I was dancing around in one spot until Jen said, "You need to pee or something?"

"Well, I need to check on the horses." Jonah kissed me on top of my head, then he walked over to Jen, who was digging in the cupboard.

"Jen." I screamed. "Behind you. Behind you."

I was laughing so hard that I fell to the floor. Jen seemed to be pretending that she couldn't see Great-grandfather, Jonah "Right there," I managed to squeak out in between laughter and breath. Jonah kissed her on top of her head. "Mom. What's the matter with this kid?"

Returning to her cupboard digging. "You better check her out, maybe she's got sunstroke or something."

I wiped the tears off and tried to hold my laughter down. My stomach hurt from laughing so hard. I looked at Jen and then back to Mom and Jonah. Mom went to open the kitchen door. "I'll need you girls to help me get the clothes on the line."

Jonah winked at me and kissed Mom on the cheek and stepped outside onto the porch.

"Aww, Mom. I already helped get the clothes on the line this morning," Jen moaned.

The clink of the wooden spoon on the pitcher beat a half time percussion against the pounding in my ears. I felt odd – a floating feeling like I was a ghost in a weird dream. Mom touched my shoulder and I jumped like our cat Missy did when I woke her. She walked to the counter, opened a drawer and took out an apron which she tied on me.

"Come on Jen," she said. "Let's all get the dry clothes and hang up the next load."

Jen poured herself a half glass of juice and swallowed it in two gulps. "This pitcher better be full when we get back in here."

The three of us went outside. The porch was shaded and had shelving for boots and shoes. On top of the shelves were the plastic baskets, two empty ones and two full of wet clothes and sheets. Jen took her pink apron from a smaller wooden basket that held all the wooden clothespins and two aprons, Jen's pink one and another green apron.

Mom tied the green on. She pulled me closer and filled the pockets of my apron with clothespins. Jen stomped down the steps with an empty basket crushed to her hip and went down to the clothes-line.

Mom took the wooden carving out of her skirt pocket.

"This is me when I was your age. Mooshom Jonah carved it for me. He died just before you were born." She knelt down to look into my eyes. "I've always needed it to see him. I can't believe you can see him without it." She shook her head and smiled. " He's a very good storyteller, you know."

"Was that really him? Isn't he dead?"

"Yes. Does that scare you?"

I looked down at the whitewashed floor of the porch, biting my thumbnail.

"Helloooo. I thought we were *all* supposed to be taking the clothes off the line," Jen yelled from the side of the house. "Gawd, I should get extra allowance for this."

We both laughed.

Mom tucked the carving back into her apron pocket and she went down the steps and around the corner of the house.

I grabbed an empty basket as I looked out across the farmyard, it seemed that everything was brighter. It seemed as though I was looking through a ViewMaster and the picture card in it was of my yard. And me, I was holding the Viewmaster right up to the sun.

Word From Our Sponsor

Breakdown of the structure of the traditional family
What kind of man will I grow to be tomorrow
Learned behavior from my boxed in babysitter,
As a twig is bent, so shall the tree grow
For this, I was birthed to live and breath
But never to leave this bright iridescent glow

Diverting my narrowed scope of perception
Dulling, numbing and blind
All but total sensory deprivation
Attention focused on colors and blinking lights
Whatever happened to the forgotten art of conversation
During this word from our sponsor, I have no time to live my life

That Shiny Little Orange And Yellow Fish

He glides back and forth
in his little world
With only a little
scuba guy for company
This is his universe,
this little bowl
He has no abstract thought
or long term memory.

If he's been happy for
thirty seconds then,
He's been happy all his life
and no further can he see
Corral rocks,
and shells
provide him with the
illusion that he is free.

My Roots In Retrospect And Metaphor

Once, a long time ago
My great, great, great grandmother
Strong
Proud
And unbroken. With love,
Fed her brood from her
Strong, unbreakable breast
To raise a
Lost
Hungry
And weak child
Who would have died
Only to have him take
From his brother's mouth
Food that was given freely
To a child out of love.

And she became ill.

Once, a long time ago
My great, great, great grandfather
Strong
Proud
And unbroken. In friendship,
Relaxed a clenched and
Strong, unbreakable fist
To extend an open
Hand to pick up a
Lost
Hungry
And weak man
Who could not stand
Only to have his fingers

Broken one at a time
On the hand extended
To a man in need.

And he became bitter.

Ignorance and Indians

A while back, a good friend of mine shared a rather amusing anecdote about a conversation he had with a Canadian within forty-eight hours of arriving in Vancouver on a work visa. He took in a local café and being a friendly, outgoing individual, struck up a conversation with one of the locals. The local was confused from the outset and she became increasingly so as they continued. You see, his thick East-London accent (at least in her mind) didn't jive with his facial features and dark complexion. She asked where he was from.

After a few moments, she seemed relieved. "So you're East Indian?"

Now it was my friend's turn to be confused. "Ah, no. Actually, my mother is Persian and my father is originally from western India."

"Yeah, so you're an East Indian", she said with an ingratiating smile. "No," he said while wondering if she misunderstood. "I was born in England..." he began and painted a detailed picture of his background.

The confusion in her eyes was replaced by a glaze and then, of all things, amusement. "Yes," she said with a patronizing pat on his forearm, " but you're still an East Indian."

She rose from her chair and left him staring at the withering foam of his latte. *So much for the legendary liberal reputation Canadians have abroad.* My friend's bewilderment at this odd bit of classification didn't last long as he soon met people who were more enlightened they helped fill in the cultural gaps.

The East Indian label is an acceptable one to most Canadians, but is the furthest thing from being liberal. In fact, it serves only to keep the racist mentality of mainstream consciousness alive and well. While some repercussions of colonization have gone the way of the dodo bird (or the vast herds of buffalo), so much lingers on like a festering sore.

East Indian. . . east of what? East of England that's what. But hey, we live in a post-colonial era, eh?

Working in several elementary schools on the West Coast as an Aboriginal Liaison, I am privy to all sorts of glaring examples of hypocrisy. The majority of students in these communities are of Indian ancestry and the sense of bewilderment my friend had experienced is often mirrored in their faces as well. In truth, many see themselves and their relations as Indians or Indo-Canadians. The vast majority of the non-Indian students, Aboriginal students included, call them Hindus, Towel Heads and Pakies, among other inaccurate appellations and insulting slurs. Ironically, only a small fraction have immigrated from Pakistan. The population in this area are predominantly Sikh from Punjab that lies in western India.

My job consists of many things, including academic support and the cultural enrichment of the Aboriginal population. I tend to spend a great deal of energy bridging cultural gaps among students, teachers, administrators and parents. Having grown up in redneck country in southern Alberta, I always imagined relations between cultures would be more amicable elsewhere. I soon discovered this was not the case. The racism was frighteningly subversive. Even more frightening was the level of internalized racism in the Aboriginal community.

Politically speaking, old regional rivalries between Indigenous nations have largely dissolved. War parties no longer stalk the waterways and trade routes. Sadly, I have met individuals who still harbor prejudice against their former enemies, although they are thousands of kilometers from their homelands. The dividing lines and reshaping of territory imposed by the governments of Canada echoes in our collective hearts and minds. Status vs. non-Status vs. C-31 vs. Métis. Child vs. Parent vs. Elder. Traditional vs. Christian. Policies and legislation forced upon our ancestors were designed not only to subjugate and oppress, but to focus our energies inward, against each other and against ourselves. Most of the Aboriginal students I encounter have only a vague idea of which nation(s) they hail from. Their cultural identity, eroded by colonization, has been replaced with apathy, shame, misplaced resentment and anger – and worst of all, self-destruction.

While enormous efforts are being made across Turtle Island to reinstall pride in ourselves, stereotypes and misunderstanding persist on both sides of the divide. This is nothing new. What *is* relatively new are the negative energies being directed at immigrants, people of color, who have come to share our lands. Ironically, a popular line of attack is aimed toward the retention of languages and cultural beliefs. Demanding that these families drop all ties and become assimilated Canadians is a tragic case of social projection. Perhaps even more ironic is that these people are awakening from their own colonial nightmares. In misdirecting our energies in this way, we strengthen those bonds we struggle to break. Why don't we focus on commonalities and understanding our differences?

I have an advantage in addressing this issue with students since I come from a long line of mixed blood marriages that date back to the mid-16th century, some that include traditional enemies. Somewhere between Cartier's abductions of sons and daughters and Champlain's war on the beaver, my Aboriginal and French ancestors began intermarrying among the nations along what is now known as the St. Lawrence seaway. Inspired by the arrogance and ignorance of Columbus the European fortune hunters who came to the northern reaches of Turtle Island carried on with the tradition of mistranslation, misunderstanding and haughty indifference toward the original names of the peoples, places and cultural practices of this land.

My history lessons open with the word *Aboriginal*. Many of us are fixated on the prefix *ab* as having negative connotations: as in *ab*normal, *ab*ominable or *ab*horrent. Yet, the prefix has neither positive nor negative implications; it is merely Latin for "from". The rest of the word is self-explanatory. Now step into imaginary birchbark canoes and paddle along the ancient waterways my ancestors traveled. Beginning with the Mi'kmaw (Mi'kmaq), the students and I travel upriver into the lands of the Wendat (Huron), the Màmìwininì (Algonquin), the Kanienkehaka (Mohawk), the Anishnabek (Ojibway) and up to James Bay into Kenistenaag (Cree) territory. The latter is a prime example of mistranslation as Kenistenaag became Kristinaux, then morphed into Cris and finally anglicized to Cree. Having shared the rich diversity of my Métis background with the students, it allows not only for an alterNative angle of the early years of contact, conflict and trade, but as a springboard into constructive discourse surrounding over 500 years of race relations.

There is no arguing that the underlying motives of greed and manifest destiny of the European forays into the New World have warped the world-view of both the colonizer and colonized. Resentment and hatred thrive on both sides. History has always painted the dominant culture in the best possible light. Throughout written history, very little survives in the way of contemporary criticism. This form of oppression has plagued relations between the

Aboriginal Peoples of Turtle Island and our neighbors for centuries. Canadians generally see themselves as an enlightened society, the voice of reason in global affairs, promoting equality, democracy and advocacy of human rights. Having swept the nastier side of our history under the carpet of international humanitarianism and universal health care makes it near impossible for the average Canadian to accept Aboriginal Peoples true history.

Maintaining the status quo has been a priority long before the nation of Canada was formed. American tactics in Native relations through history are often criticized by Canadians as wantonly violent, callous and even savage. The difference between these two *powers that be* is that Canadian authorities have been more history conscious and ultimately more subversive in their dealings. Any attempts to reassert the autonomy and sovereignty of the Indigenous peoples have been met, with submission, by starvation, by slander, by biological agents and by threatened or active violence.

What has really changed since the Indian Wars of the eastern woodlands, since the massacre at Wounded Knee or the Rebellions of 1870 and 1885 on the plains? The confrontations at Kanesatake and Gustafson Lake are only exceptional in that the media was there to enforce and therefore dictated a little caution on the part of the Canadian authorities. Violence was still the outcome and was once again initiated by the non-Native side of the barricades. The truth is still filtered and distorted to paint the warriors as frothing, unreasonable militants.

Once a savage, always a savage, eh?

If we can dispel the old enmities within ourselves and between nations we can continue to quash stereotypes and prejudice in a far more effective manner. Our collective voice will grow in strength and volume. The trickle of truth and justice that currently flows will inevitably feed into a mighty river. Indian resistance against English dominance under Mahatma Ghandi is an inspiring starting point. The strength and pride of regional nations will bring us together as One Great Nation. Perhaps, by focusing on our commonalities with the other colonized peoples of the world instead of resenting them as we are conditioned to, together we can decolonize Turtle Island. Finally our attentions can shift as they should, to restoring the sacred balance and healing of Mother Earth.

Alone, our struggle will flounder. Together, the river of change will be undamable, flowing into a harmonious future. By honoring the spirit of our ancestors who initially agreed to share this bountiful land, perhaps we can move towards this end sooner rather than later. The *powers that be* must also honour this and acknowledge the wrong-doings and injustices of the past and present. Perhaps then we will move into a future in which the Great Peace of the Haudenosaunee (Iroquois) Confederacy, the template for democracy around the world, will reign for seven generations and beyond.

Fort George Island

Minshtook,*
On warm summer days
We walk through
Your tall grasses
To sit under
Your giant spruce trees
And talk about
Far away places.

Minshtook,
From your sandy shores
We place our canoes in the water
And rock to a gentle rhythm
With our paddles
To nearby places
For fish, animals, birds and berries.

Your *neepsee** provides
Secret places for embracing lovers
While others scoop pails of water
To carry home for washing and cooking.

Over the mouth of your mighty river
The reds and oranges of the setting sun
Casts a glow of warmth upon watching faces
Before they settle down for the night
In the yellow glow of kerosene lamps,
Candlesticks, and fireplaces.

Minshtook,
You set my spirit free
To travel the Chisasibi
And salt water coastline
Of James Bay.

**Minshtook* = Island
**neepsee* = under brush, willows

Alone

There is a creek, full of fish and other
animals, she is full of life
the creek runs through the valley
meandering along ponderosa pines
alone, yet full because she is
married to the earth and carries life
within her currents

as the creek rushes over pebbles
and streams over boulders
she sings a song of many melodies

a deer with mighty antlers drinks deep
he is alone, magnificent
in all his glory walking over the earth
with delicate steps
to visit the creek on occasion
to arch his neck down
with gentle lips he sucks life
to stream down his throat

satisfied, he turns to disappear
into the forest, free
to take whichever path he chooses, leaving her

alone… to trace over again and again
a set course, carrying life
within her wake
and songs of the earth.

Indian Princess:
Who I am

I am observation, sexual stimulation, no justification
I am reduced, disjoined, destructive and corrosive
I am transfixed by my beauty and my brain
I am immovable
I am repeatedly revived by moistened breath
I am flowing vibe motioning my hands for creation
I am with religious persuasion, blood, omitted
I am nurturer to Shifting White Cloud baby

I am not a stagnant Indian Princess
I am not miscellaneous or invisible
I am unforgettably her and will never
        try and change who I am
        to match society's prototype.

Section 2

The Grandmothers are Dancing in my Hair

time holds itself around the middle and laughs

this is where it all begins
that moment   that glorious moment
drives through a rainbow in her car
blossomed close
and blood earth red
heavy and upright
holding many trees

on the other side
there is a whisper on the wet warm ground
imagine the sound
the round water sound
inside rain
                        if you go there
                        you'll be
                        eternity

After the rain, a small spotted eagle, her feathers spread like butter, ready for bannock and tea. An urban eagle pretending to fit in and looking for a piece of the pie. Small spotted eagle meets a woman on the street. At first she thinks this woman is albino crow on account of the shine on the car she's straddling, and remembering somewhere in her something about crows and where the food is, she hovers without hesitation, hunger leading her around like one of those dogs she's seen on strings, happy to sniff at the edges of life.

they came on the voice of fire

it is said
long time ago
seven young women
michahai yokuts women
two-spirit women
whose respect
for their parents
their grandparents
do not question
in their youth
the promise
to the parents
the grandparents
of beautiful young men
to marry
in the good way
of the time

with age
time slows
like wind on stone
after a storm
whose water washes
cleanses
softens
their delicate intent
unwinds
unable to love
their husbands

as women do

seven young women
put onion in their hair
their clothes
their breath
their beds
to keep their men
away

the years pass
in stillness
and still
seven young women
search
for a way

and so it is said
seven young women
pray
fast
six full days
their bones
parched and raining
fire
of power
like no other

away
a way to escape
from married life
once
and for all
time

two singers
entwined seers
in one person
to see spirits female
interpreters of dreams
as she to male
as he spirits male mediators
to be to female healers
as he
as she

and after they fast
six full days
seven young women
make their way
to a cliff
so high
above the trees
their moons
go
their breath
slow

and there
on ropes
of eagle down
six young women
go
their movement
slow

eagle down
rises
to carry
six young women

become
pleiades
of taurus

many hundreds
of star sisters
hidden from six young
women
the ordinary
human visible
eye protect
surround

in time
seven young husbands even celestial
follow six young women
do not wish
seven young husbands seven young
husbands
become near
taurus
where
aldebaran
red star
whose gift
of brilliance holds

one young woman
the youngest
remains
with mother earth
transforms
to stone

This stone is mother to a small round stone held here until the time is right. This is how this story is told to small spotted eagle by her grandmother, who is told by her grandmother, who is told by her grandmother is how small spotted eagle is told in her language.

Waiting…

Indians can wait out anything.

We can wait out lovers
marriages
disease

We can even wait out Jesus.

We wait out bad coffee
cold showers
a beating
a rape
a lie.

The queens of our nations
we wait them out too.

The white man usually gets first crack
but we'll get her
when she returns to the home
we've circled for years.

We can wait out winter
seasons of deceit
nightmares
our lives…

Birth

Birth beckons me to cum
She wraps her cedar legs around my heart and squeezes hard
till she almost chokes my spirit out of my body
Until I give in to her labor pains
I begin to smell the stench of her rotten afterbirth
Sweet tangy sour and rotten gag caught in my gut throat
I threaten to puke all over the truth spirit has laid before me

Birth has dislodged all that was residing and stewing beneath my
salmon skin
The memories etched into my dna the generational trauma flowing in
my blood the gifts
sleeping in my bones and the gloryful bliss tattooed to my forehead
I breathe deep and full and know I can't stop this birth
There is no way to escape the rim of fire
I breathe belly again and surrender to the unknown mystery

I go deep into the darkness to find bright light to create my new
dream
I wrestle and scrap it out hard with my demons with my parasites
with my monsters with my shadows with my hidden self
They and I become one and the same of dirt of spirit of everything primal
Bile blood bones snot puke shit piss mucus sweat
All mixed together being pushed out my pores like slimy play dough
For the earth to absorb transform shape shift and dissolve into tiny
healing crystal crackles

I hear the call of cedar babies and I stand up and let my womb be
softened and warmed butterscotch brown by their presence
After many sleepless nights I unlock myself from the steel cage I got
frozen into at conception
I walk out of my history
I resurrect my Sex Goddess
I hurl all the heavy fur blankets connecting me to woman pain off
my back in a huge fury that spans generations of Kwakwaka'wakw

women who rage to be free to be wild to remember who they are
I take one last breath rich and low from the depths of my swamp and
push with all my might to let
GOOOOOOOOOOOOOOOOOOOOOOOOOOOOOOOOOOOOOOO

Energy

Energy is everything
Movement and tunnels shape into doorways caves into windows
mushrooms into rainbows cotton candy into purple stew
It carries all the stories of what's gone on
It knows ALL

Us, we carry our stories with us on the curve of our spine
in our lower lip
on the tips of our toes
on our right breast
in the texture of our hair
along our left jaw bone
and deep inside our throat

Energy shifts emotions/Energy movements situations/Energy brings forth action
Energy emerges the truth/Energy unfolds experiences/Energy leads us to discover clues about our life's bliss/Energy blows us into our dark spots and keeps us there until we find courage to become our magnificence/Energy brings the toxins in to our body and takes them out/Energy creates destroys rebuilds transforms and heals

Energy tingles and shivers the intuition to guide us to safety within our own body's Big House
away from danger into glory away from blurriness into color away from dark into beauty away from fear into richness away from sadness into belly laughter away from rage into pleasure away from pain into truth away from illusion into vitality away from chaos into sweetness away from deprivation into succulence away from shame into gorgeousness away from guilt into dance away from intellect into imagery away from control into rhythm away from judgment into enlightenment away from concrete into innocence away from horror into purity away from rigidity into the miracle away from projection into the NOW

Energy is all
It moves it shapes
it brings life it kills
it reinvents it creates
it births it grows
it nurtures it hones
it depletes it nourishes

It's in out up down under above over around and through
It's all the little spots in between
It's the density that keeps us intact
It's the tool we have to guide protect heal truth tell transform rebuke
embrace accept and enjoy
Energy is...

The Grandmothers are Dancing in My Hair

The Grandmothers are dancing in my hair
They're weaving and braiding a waltz
of warmth and sadness of secrets and rainbows
Slow. Suave. Molassy. Electric.
Each thick strand of blue-black hair
A world stage
for Grandmother
to belt her body story out for the universe to taste
Bright vivacious colors flying, twirling, gyrating their pitter-patter onto scalp floor
Grandmothers' full, round hips shake dresses a – float, shake dresses a-high
Grandmothers' hands tease, play, jostle,
tummy laughter to rise, riSE, RISE
onto soft, brown clouds of Goddess memory
Grandmother taunts, provokes, and pulls strands of bliss
for every Grandmother that ever dared to dance
for every daughter, aunty, cousin, niece, friend, sister
who couraged to remember
her Rhythm
The Grandmothers are dancing in my hair

Tree Dance

in the darkness of the night
a lone tipi lights the faces
of children watching their mother
watching their father
stepping lightly in a circle
around a fire
in rhythm to his drum

sparks fly into the air
through the smoke vent
into the star lit sky

two rivers north
a tall dome shaped
tent shakes to a low chant
visions of migrating caribou
traverse the eyes
of a *medew*
southwest over the land
to behold the eyes of a hunter

nihii nihii
shaking tent has returned
to the hearts of the people
so has *medewewin*
sun dance
winter dance
potlatch

hey hey
the drum strikes hard
across the land
and the sound of music
fills my soul
bigger than the sound of music
in the Grand Hall
at the Museum of Civilization

different drums unite
as the grass dance unfolds
across the prairies
as the winter dance echoes
in the mountains

shawl dancers furl fringes
along rivers stretching over land
languages flow from mother tongues
speaking a past into the present

from ocean to ocean
rhythms voice a people
strong with the will for survival
swaying in time to the sound
of the wind and the rain
through pine cedar spruce cottonwood
aspen willow spread their branches to the sky

medew = shaman
nihii nihii = yes yes, as used in chant
medewewin = medicine lodge society

Contours

I am stuck in the
present and future
television life of
different strips of
made up words
broken words
bouncing off
satellite stations
threatening to
fling me into
another mindless
foreign dimension
other than the one
I already
struggle to escape.

Mindless
gut cursed
surreal words
left behind
spattered
on gritty greasy
pavement in the alley
ricochet higher and higher
up walls, echoing off
vertical multiples
of plain grey
cement blocks encasing
steel strips
while I roll along
strips on wheels down
strips upon strips
of pavement strapping
the surface of the earth
while molds of hard metal
cars threaten to

drive me out of my mind.

Aimlessly I wander
over parallel
upon parallel of
pavement, neon,
red and green lights,
until, in the distance,
peeking through
a tree imprisoned
by vertical multiples
of post-Neolithic
slabs of cement,
a strip of glimmering
clear blue light
beckons me
to come.

I respond to
the clear blue light.
Dead ends block
my way,
I backtrack
sharp corners
slipping over
garbage leaking
out of metal,
pot holes contain
no flowers,
people surge up
from the ground
from subways like
sardines from a rusty can.

Trembling, I break
through the greasy
metal mess.
Before me shines

the clear blue wall
of shimmering light.

Below the blue,
tall golden yellow
grass seed heads
swallow me into
waves of warm
undulating dances
to twirl me about
through streams
of rays that
bathe me in light
and drown out the
vertical multitudes
of cement buildings
that I have left behind.

My soul fills
into the freedom
I longed for.

Twirling and twirling
I leave behind
parallels of strips
of hard concrete lines
to fall into yellow
soft contours,
to warm
black earth,
to stare at the
clear blue sky.

Falling into recesses
of the past
in dreamful sleep
to fields of
flowery shore

upon flowery shore where
blanket soft heads
lead my longing
into warm nurturing
lines of contours
of shore line
and strip hard metal cars
from my mind to

nestle into
contours
upon contours
of bright yellow
petals to face the
new dawn ascending
from the horizon.

The sun
beckons me to
follow half
its journey back
to the time when
animals and people
wore leather,
and braided strips
of truth
into one mind
to follow
the natural laws of nature.

Essentialized Blindness

You can't see me
with your essentialized eyes
I have no braids
or feathers

You can't see my spirit
my wings spread wide
chest full of pride
and my head lifted high

You can't see my power
as I peek from the woods
watching you
attacking your weakness

You can't see my people
bound to the land
through blood relations
and speaking our tongue

You can't see my determination
it is all around you
as you step onto my land
looking for braids and feathers

You can't see the Indian
because of all the brown skinned people
standing in the way

Lingering Question

You are in the wind
I can feel you
pushing me forward
making me stronger
You force me to stand up straight

You are in the sunset
I can see you
hugging me with your last ray
allowing your sister starlight second watch
You bring me sleep

You are in the alpine meadow
I can smell you
drifting me across you
giving me a warm bed
You allow me to dream

You are in the salmon
I can taste you
providing me with protein
letting me be full
You provide a method of growth

You are in the eagle's voice
I can hear you
trailing behind your voice
blazing a new trail
You give me a direction

You are in my spirit
I can't breath without you
making my heart pump faster
causing my voice to stutter
my legs as I stand with you

You are part of my family
You complete my being

For I am home

Red Willow Baskets

I plan my escape while nestled in threadbare flannel sheets
listening to crickets scrape their song

taunts me with harsh beauty

My bare feet wander over hard paths carved into
the heaving sides of a glittering snake whose
tongue flickers out to taste the souls it will devour

life struggles between the cracks of diamond scales

I run from a pitiful man who smells of piss and booze
my hand clenching dimes he demanded from me
as sweat drips from my brow to splatter on the sidewalk

dries fast under the hot sun

White lies send me across a sienna sky
sending my spirit flying over concrete spires that
spew sulphur clouds into blue paradise

cries from white buffalo woman

My escape has not gone unnoticed
My captors have not given up

I live cloaked in fog
weaving red willow baskets for my grandchildren

Silent Cries at Lullabies

Swinging from a shoelace,
That hangs from neither shoe nor boot,
Face painted up with grief.
I smile deaths wide tooth grin,
And stare through vacant eyes,
Shouting silent cries at lullabies that never end.

Festival of The Dead

I enter the bar, sit back, kick my feet up and order a beer.
Soon I am peering around thinking, how very much these
people remind me of an infestation, like maggots in the
rotting meat of a corpse.

I continue drinking and taking in everything visually.
I notice the phone booth is glowing red,
giving off a sickly aura of drug and sex related calls.
still I continue drinking,

Drip,
Drip,
Drip,

Ahhhhh, my only companion this night.
So lecherous, like a liquid succubae, so soothing, so nice.
it leaves me wanting more while sucking out my soul.
Nothing more than a shadow of myself I exit the bar,
Like a thousand phantom dogs running fiery circles through
my soul.
I lash out at everything.
I recall thinking this must be the festival of the dead

Section 3

Family Gathering

Revised *Its'ka*

Chapter One

Spring, 1983.

Aunt Emily Kato is standing behind the guardrail at Toronto's airport hailing exuberantly as I exit the baggage area with my cart piled high with luggage. There is a twinkly-eyed bear of a man behind her holding a camera and ready to shoot. Beside Aunt Emily, barely recognizable, is a striking, elegant woman in a dark business suit. Is that Baby Anna? What a surprise! The oversized teenager I last saw in southern Alberta is not much in evidence. She is taller than I remember. The sharply slanted eyes and high cheekbones, I do remember Anna Makino. One hand is on her hip, the other high in greeting. I wave back. The flash pops once, twice, three times.

"You made it! You actually made it!"A laughing Anna looks as though she belongs on the cover of a business magazine.

"Finally!"

Aunt Emily's mock exasperation is rich, throaty. There is a density in her voice. More than that, there's a density in her whole being which makes people defer to her. She grabs my carry-on with one hand and unceremoniously wraps my arm in the other as she nods her introductions.

"Naomi, William Schellenberg."

"Hello, Naomi." A wide friendly grin greets me.

So this is the William Schellenberg I've been hearing about. A wounded, talented man of the streets who has become her devoted friend.

"William? He's demented," she'd say, "but he's brilliant. He's like a big dog that hasn't been properly trained, you know."

I nod at him over my shoulder as I'm being dragged ahead. "Hello and thanks," I say as he takes the cart and shambles along behind us.

William Schellenberg at first glance is an affable man, casually dressed in baggy jeans and sweater, a reddish grey-tinged beard thick and ragged, clearly not an overly fastidious person. He is close to Aunt Emily's age. Early sixties perhaps. Mid fifties? It's hard to guess. No-one believes me when I tell them I am well over forty.

"You Asians," they say shaking their heads. "You don't age."

Not true of course. Two years ago when Aunt Emily officially gasped her way over the hill and received an old age citizen's card she said with chagrin and disbelief, "I'm a pensioner. Good grief."

My mother's younger sister is a militant *nisei*, a second-generation born in Canada woman of Japanese ancestry, headstrong and outspoken. Most children of the *issei* that I know are outwardly gentle, polite and quiet. Aunt Em is decidedly not.

My other aunt, Aya Obasan, raised my brother and me. She was as different from Aunt Emily as earth is from air, as the roots of a tree are from branches. Obasan was a typical *issei*: silent, indomitable, fed by an underground stream of an ancient culture. When Obasan died, Aunt Emily tried to persuade me to pack up my little life on the prairies and move to be with her in Toronto.

"Just for a couple of months if you want. At least try it out," she said. "We have to stick together now, you know. There's only you and me and your brother left."

In the end, it wasn't so much her insistence as my own drooping limbs that uprooted me. Life had become stagnant in southern Alberta.

"I know you'll miss the big sky but you'll grow to love the big smog. You won't regret it," she said.

I had my qualms while flying over the city, looking down from the tiny window at the colorless urban grid, with miles and miles of buildings like tombstones. Toronto was a gigantic cemetery.

The airport is a great grey hubbub of cars, taxis, limos, buses, and strangers lined along the sidewalks, with carts of baggage and people getting in and out of vehicles.

"Glad you're here, Naomi," William says.

I help him tie down the trunk of Aunt Emily's small car to keep it from flapping open. He takes a box of books and squeezes into the back seat with Anna. I get in the front passenger seat, jerking it forward to give him leg room. Aunt Emily's description of him as a large dog seems apt. English sheepdog. A hairy man. The car lurches into the traffic.

"You okay back there, William?" asks Aunt Emily.

"I'll live," he said squirming under the heavy box on his lap.

"Naomi, I hear you two knew each other in Alberta?" His voice has the modulated baritone of a singer or a radio announcer.

"Baby Anna?"

I turn to discover that his intense gaze and thick inquiring eyebrows might belie my first impression of an easy-going man.

"I've known Anna Makino since the day she was born. How long since you were in Granton, Anna? Fifteen, twenty years?" he asked.

"Something like that," answers Anna.

Anna Makino, like my brother Stephen and so many of the brightest and best, left the prairies right after high school and never looked back. We, who knew her as a baby, saw the hunger right from the beginning. People often said she and Stephen would go far.

Toronto is going to take some getting used to. We are speeding along the freeway in the fast lane, passing most of the drivers that are also tearing along. It seems that we will get to our destinations without an accident. We exit onto Spadina Avenue and enter the constricted car-clogged streets of the city's core. Aunt Emily's house on the north edge of Chinatown is a solid, square two-story brick with two fireplaces – one upstairs that's never used. The room she offers me is a former study, a sunny addition beside the kitchen.

"Couldn't get a pin in here last month," Aunt Emily says as we haul my worldly belongings into the pleasant space. "I knew you wouldn't be able to stand all my old furniture."

She gestures at the freshly painted and carpeted room. "So?"

There is a wall length closet, a south window above a radiator, a pull down shade on a glass door that opens onto a long cedar deck that runs out to a ramshackle garden of wildflowers enclosed by a high fence.

Sunshine. Privacy.

"It's perfect, Aunt Em."

"It's a miracle, actually," Anna says. "You should've seen what we carted out of this room."

"Well, that was the deal. An empty room," Aunt Emily says, her finger printing the letters M T in the air.

The one time Aunt Emily visited me in my spartan little house in Alberta, she was shocked at how little I owned. "You'd peel your skin off and get rid of it if it wasn't stuck to you," She'd said. I'm quite unlike Aunt Emily or Obasan in that one respect. I'm not a keeper or collector of things. Perhaps it's a reaction to the clutter in which I grew up.

Some of Aunt Emily's boxes sit unpacked in her new study upstairs, a handsome oak-paneled room with a blocked off fireplace, a floppy couch and built-in bookshelves. It's a former guest room where William once stayed. Dozens of other boxes have been dumped in the basement – a lifetime of letters, notes, pictures, clippings and stacks of the familiar old mimeographed *Church News* that Aunt Emily had kept over the years and was our *issei* minister, Nakayama-sensei's life-long effort to keep people in touch. During and after World War II, the only social nourishment available to thousands of isolated people were his tiny tidbits of news – a baby born in Golden, B.C., Mrs. Oka of Raymond, ill, the Takahashi children winning sports awards. It seems everyone knew each other then.

Aunt Emily's theory is that people blow away in the wind like topsoil or tumble-weeds unless their roots remain entwined. "Newsletters are like glue," she says when she gives us the guided tour. "Hearts can shrivel up, you know. If the will to connect withers, whole countries shrivel up. It could happen to Canada. Do you ever think the CBC, the railway, our health system – these kinds of things – if they'd unravel, you know, we'd unravel. You westerners ought to understand. Alberta and Saskatchewan farmers, for instance. And Native people – planting corn and not ploughing it all up, for heaven's sake."

She pats a stack of boxes beside the filing cabinet in her new study. "My junk. You probably think it's junk, Nomi, but…"

"Well, you've got a big house here."

"It's a national treasure, Emily. These papers," William says somberly, "Are the Japanese-Canadian Dead-Sea scrolls."

Aunt Emily laughs and claps him on the back appreciatively. There's an ease and a collegiality William exudes that softens the edge of Aunt Emily's bluntness.

"When I was a kid," Anna says, "I couldn't have imagined this country unraveling. Couldn't have imagined it."

She's thumbing through one of Aunt Emily's many ever-evolving old newsletters. Her Nisei News had started off as a weekly bulletin in the fifties but became a monthly, then a quarterly and finally dwindled into an occasionally. These days it's been reduced to the status of an annual Christmas letter.

"You really think Canada's disappearing?"

Aunt Emily shrugs. "Are we disappearing? Does a Japanese-Canadian community exist? What do you think, Nomi?"

"Does it matter?"

"Oh oh," William chuckles. "Does it matter! Watch out there, Naomi."

I should have known better than to be so flippant I think as Aunt Emily groans and rolls her eyes. I'll need to tip-toe around these booby-trapped questions in the future.

After Anna and William leave, Aunt Emily and I sit on the pull-out bed in the living room drinking sleepy-time tea and munching Japanese crackers and melon slices. We're looking through a pile of albums with photographs I've never seen. Aunt Emily as a little girl before she wore glasses, with a big floppy bow in her hair. My lovely young mother Mari, in front the peach tree beside our house with me, a well-wrapped baby in her arms. Stephen, my big brother, is a shy toddler peeking out from behind Mother's skirt.

"And this one's in Stanley Park," Aunt Emily says.

Sweet Grandma Nakane sits on a picnic blanket with the newly-weds, Aya Obasan and Uncle. I remember Obasan saying once with a laugh that she married Uncle to please Grandma Nakane. And there in front of a lodge with their car is skinny Grandma Kato, elegant in pearls and lace. All these, Aunt Emily says, were from our "paradise lost" Vancouver years. It is a feast for my starving eyes.

"Oh yes, and this!" Aunt Emily says pulling out a brown-paper parcel from the stack. "Now this is really old." It is addressed in her strong youthful handwriting to Mr. Isamu Nakane, P.O. Box 461, Granton, Alberta.

"You were mailing this to us?"

"Oh that was years ago. Years and years. Do you remember – no you wouldn't remember. Open it, Nomi. It's yours."

She unwraps the crackly dry paper and hands me a rectangular black album about one and a half hand spans long and one hand span high, bound by a black and brown cord. It looks to be exactly the same as Obasan's old album. Inside, inscribed in silver ink are the only two Japanese characters I recognize the letters for 'inside' and 'root.' Naka - ne. My surname.

"How... where did you get this?"

"It's been sitting here, waiting for you I guess. Like Grandma

Nakane, sitting there, just sitting there on that cot. I'll never forget it."

It was rainy as usual that day in 1942 Aunt Emily recalled. She'd had a cold and didn't want to take her germs to the crowded exhibition grounds in Vancouver where people were being held before getting shipped away. But the children were sick and some elderly people were particularly sick. She had her father's doctor-bag with her, full of tins of stomach medicine.

"All those women, all those children, all that bewilderment. And then – it was in the livestock building.

I recognized her from about thirty feet away and I thought, *What on earth is SHE doing here! She is supposed to be visiting in Saltspring*. And she didn't have anything with her except her *furoshiki* and, of all things, this old album. I'll never forget that stare, that blank look. She didn't know who I was. No idea. I don't think she even knew there was a war on."

"And she gave this to you?"

"When she finally recognized me. Yes. Furtively. She pushed it into Papa's bag."

Dear Grandma Nakane. I barely remember her except that she was always smiling. And now, after all these absent years, in Aunt Emily's house a pictorial record of her family in Japan. I hardly dared touch it.

"And you want to know why I finally didn't mail it? Why?"

Aunt Emily gestures impatiently, "Because your uncle didn't want it. That's right. He didn't want it. When I told him I'd send it, he said to me, he said, '*Mo ii.*' You know? 'It's enough. That's what he said."

Mo ii. The past is the past. Never mind. It's finished. It doesn't matter. Don't bother yourself. *Mo ii*. He said this when I'd massaged his shoulders enough. Now good. That's enough. Or when he didn't want another bowl of rice. It is one of the all purpose phrases that could be said in appreciation, in resignation, in anger or in irritation.

The photographs from Japan are almost entirely of strangers. I don't recognize any of the relatives – at least I presume they're relatives. Would the old woman seated in front of a large thatch-roofed house be my great great-grandmother? She has a round moon-shaped face like Grandma Nakane's.

Aunt Emily doesn't have a clue, though she points out a young mother and child, saying it must be Grandma Nakane with her first-born, Uncle Isamu, my father's half-brother. It's midnight before Aunt Emily climbs the stairs to bed. I lie awake for hours, puzzling over the pictures. There's a little boy who looks a little like Stephen.

I'm a tumbleweed in Toronto, thinking – a jumbled mesh of dried roots; a long way from yesterday's yesterday; a long way from water.

Old House

The photographs on the walls
leave behind their ghost imprint.
At the funeral, the eulogy slipped from me.
I found the words and thought no more of it,
until now. Because you old house
root me to the very spot
I took my first step.

Nothing will ever be the same.

Old house, with your crooked windows,
sagging floors, leaking roof.
Listen.
I lay up half the night listening to you
storm and subside,
and storm again, carrying me
to bottles and flying dishes,
cracked skulls and silence.
Then, the gust of birthday candles,
fiddles and guitars.

It all came so fast, old house.

Tell me. How to let go? Hold back
the rising so I can get on with it,
walk through that door again,
and greet with hello, Yes, I am fine.
Life goes on. And it does,
except now that I have felt your current
you make me grab hold to steady myself.
As I push myself into another day
where I am some kind of divining rod,
snapping awake, echoing things
I can barely touch.

Old Missus En'owkin

I be born in the morning,
the night went to play on the other side of the world.
I be born in the late spring,
winter didn't know me she melted in the chinook wind.
I be born in Nicola Valley no one knew me. I be born. I be born last.
I was the last born, therefore, I heard no songs and there was no dances.
Shhhh! Don't remind me. I remember the Coldwater River it flowed away from me.
The moon. Isn't she my sister? Why does she keep her distance away from me?
Life was a blur, my memories could not keep up to me.
The Residential School stole my childhood,
there was no love, no hugs, no kisses.
My heart longed for sunshine and love, but only loneliness stared back at me.
Many times I wanted the raindrops to touch me,
but it seemed like no one knew that I breathed the same air as they did.
I crawled beneath a heavy rock, I stayed there, my self esteem was entombed in shame.
My only friends were hate and violence.
I had a lover, her name was booze.
She was strong and sometimes sweet. She was smooth and always tempting.
On her dark side, she was wicked, evil and too much for me.
She was unfaithful, without second thoughts, she went with anyone, so I left her.
I met a friend who was kind and patient.
I met a friend who gave me courage to change, gave me serenity to see myself.
I met a friend his name was Mr. Sobriety.
I walked the Red Road, with no destination in mind.
On the road I went around a corner.
In the ditch I saw something lying on it's back.
I ran to it. I asked, "Hey are you okay?"

It didn't move. It wasn't breathing. It scared me.
I gave it mouth to mouth and it revived.
I helped it to it's feet. I stared at it.
I realized it was my inner child then we walked down the road.
It was mid nineties, no it wasn't a hot summer.
It was 1995. I left my home the Nicola Valley.
I entered the Okanagan Territory.
I walked for miles and miles.
I asked myself, "What am I doing so far away from home?"
No one knows me. What am I searching for?
I was walking on the beach, I came upon an old lady.
She sat beside a fire. Humming a strange tune.
She was making something with her elegant fingers.
I stood in the darkness. Her back was facing me.
She stopped humming and she spoke.
"Do not be afraid young man.
Come closer. That's it. Warm yourself to the fire.
Have you eaten? Are you thirsty?"
I stepped out of the darkness. I inched my way towards the old lady.
The old lady reminded me of the grandmothers back home.
She was tiny. She had deep wrinkles on her brown face. She was dressed like the four seasons.
A white winter shawl. Spring kerchief was green.
She wore a red hot summer dress and her small feet had brown autumn moccasins.
I asked the old lady, "How did you know I was behind you?"
The old lady replied, "Ooooh! The night had thousand eyes.
I can see. I can see real good."
I asked the old lady, "Who are you?"
The old lady replied, "The people around here call me, Missus En'owkin.
I gasped an ounce of air "Missus En'owkin. Don't I know you from somewhere?"

Yes! Yes! I remember. You were that old woman in the street.
Old woman. Old woman all alone
Old woman. Old woman.
Begging for food, begging for warmth, begging for change.

Old woman got nothing because I gave you nothing. I think no one
gave you nothing.
Old woman. Old woman.
The world has turned it's back against you.
The world has kept turning and turning, the world came.
It ate away the old woman's flesh, ate away the old woman's bones,
ate away everything the old woman had.
Now, there's crumbs of flesh of delusions.
Old woman, I closed my eyes. I opened my eyes.
Old woman, I looked for you on the sidewalk. You was gone.
On the sidewalk there are empty dreams, empty hopes and empty
words for prayers.
Old woman. Old woman forgive me for not believing in you,
forgive me for not respecting my Elders."

Old Missus En'owkin stared at me for a moment.
She motioned me to sit beside her on a log.
"Young man. Young man. I believe you are sorry. Now, look up to
the sky."
I looked up. I saw a star.
The star zoomed from the east to the west.
I was awed. My mouth was open. I wondered where the star went
I asked Missus En'owkin, "What kind of star was that?"
Missus En'owkin replied, "A shooting star, young man,
a shooting star."
More curious than ever. I asked, "Who shot the shooting star?"
Missus En'owkin replied, "The Creator shot the shooting star."
Still curious. "Why did the Creator shoot the shooting star?"
Missus En'owkin stopped what she was doing. She looked at me.
"Well my young man. The Creator shot the shooting star because
people have dreams.
You understand? Listen carefully.
Sometimes, the shooting star, it goes a little ways,
that means the people goes a long ways for their dreams."
I sat on the log thinking. My thoughts swirling.
It sounds easy to have a dream. All I have to do is wish.
But! But, what happens if my dreams don't come true?
Missus En'owkin! Missus En'owkin!

What if I can't reach my dreams? What if my dream dies?
Missus En'owkin put a finger to her lips. "Shhhh. Listen to yourself.
You are doubtful. Listen to me. Listen to me.
If you can't be in two places at once
then take one day at a time.
If you can't be a virgin
then experience your life to the fullest.
If you can't be faithful
accept your mistakes.
If you can't be God
be a universe of your imagination.
If you can't be Canadian
be yourself.
If you can't be a man or a woman
be your inner child.
If you can't be age that shows on your face
be young at heart.
Young man. Young man. Are you listening?"
Yes I was listening. I heard something from the darkness.
I heard footsteps then I saw people appear in the firelight.
There was old people, young people and people with children.
I asked Missus En'owkin, "Who are these people?"
Missus En'owkin stood up, and went to the people.
She shook hands with them, she hugged them and kissed them.
Missus En'owkin turned to me. "These people are my children, they
came from far and near.
I taught my children love, we are a big family.
In the family, we are sons and daughters, brothers and sisters.
We are grandparents, uncles, aunts, husbands and wives.
I taught my children to be writers, to be artists and to be storytellers.
You my young man I want you to remember something.
I want you to visualize yourself in your mother's womb. Hear your
mother's voice."

My baby! My baby!
Soon you will be born.
Soon you will enter this world.
Oh, baby baby. I'm afraid.

I'm afraid to bring you into this world.
There's lots of hate, there's lots of violence.
Oh baby I can't bring you into this world, I'd be killing you.
Oh baby! Baby what shall I do?

Young man. Young man. Your mother loved you.
She cared for you. She was afraid of this violent world. She made a choice.
You be born in the morning. You be born in late spring. You be born in Nicola Valley.
Young man. You thought there was no songs, no dances.
I was told from the spirits of our ancestors, your mother was happy to have a son.
Your mother sang her heart out. Your mother danced with her pride.
Young man. Young man. I've been waiting for you for a long time.
I knew someday, you would show up. I have a gift for you.
My elegant fingers was doing some weaving.
I weaved your dreams, your hopes and lot of prayers.
I weaved your heart, your mind and your spirit.
"Here, take my gift young man.
From this day on, I will call you my grandson."
I took the gift from Missus En'owkin.
Tears of love rolled down my cheeks.
I gave Missus En'owkin a big hug.
As we hugged, Missus En'owkin spoke to me in a low tone.
"Some days are not born, some days will come and they will go.
What days you asked. Your childhood days, your Residential School days
Your drinking days and your healing days.
Days will come and they will go.
Days will go far into the past, far into your memories and they may never return.
Some day my grandson, you will be a storyteller.
Some day you will return, do not tell me goodbye."
I watched Missus En'owkin, she sat on the log, her elegant fingers began weaving again.
I thought she wass weaving a gift for someone else.
I went home to Nicola Valley.

I became an Indian book.
I have stories of long ago, stories of today and stories of tomorrow.
I'm an Indian book I sat on the bookshelf.
I'm an Indian book many people came
and they read my stories over and over and over.

En'owkin Centre
My Days in Nerd Land

I don't really know if I was a nerd in high school. I never thought of myself as one because I didn't spend all my time doing homework or studying. I did, however, spend a lot of time reading. I collected books and had them in boxes in my closet. When I wanted to get away from my siblings in the winter I would go behind the boxes and set up a reading space complete with pillow and blanket. In the summer when I wasn't helping Mom with young ones I'd find a place under a tree, or up in a tree, with my book. Forty years later I went back to school full time and became a nerd.

I made a promise to myself (I guess subconsciously) that I wouldn't go to school after high school unless I could study what I wanted. I found that school in the En'owkin Centre. The En'owkin Centre provided me with courses in creative writing and fine arts and helped me explore more of myself than I'd ever dreamed. I was allowed to write and read and do only that. There was no calculus or biology or Latin. There were ways to explore different mediums in fine art. I even got to take two English courses that helped me to get over a revulsion around grammar.

My reason for going to the En'owkin Centre was to find a way to get my book published. I'd been a counsellor in addictions and abuses for over seventeen years and wanted to write and publish this book. I gave Jeannette Armstrong the rough first draft. She took it to Theytus and they said they'd publish it. I went to school to publish the book and they taught me vision. I knew how to write as my teacher Beth Cuthand told me, I just didn't know how to envision it. Jeannette helped with that. The writing courses were not just fiction; they included poetry and non-fiction as well as screen and script writing. I swore to my English teacher Gerry William that I wasn't going to write essays and that I hated writing essays. When the next issue of *Gatherings* came out he emailed me and said, "I see you're writing essays Helen." He brought some laughter into a troubling day.

My book *Shaking the Rattle: Healing the Trauma of Colonization* published by Theytus in 1996, the year of my graduation from En'owkin, was my main focus at school. I had already written the non-fiction pieces and had to learn how to tighten them up and give them my voice. I had to learn about fiction writing and poetry. I'd never liked poetry since high school English classes. But these teachers and students helped me to appreciate poetry and to write it as well.

Although I had a book deadline, that didn't stop me from appreciating the fine talent and artistic ability that surrounded me while I worked. Oh, so many fine writers and wonderful artists. There was one girl – Anna Sewell – who just fascinated me with her mind. She came up with a performance piece that I still want permission to write about. It was awesome. Crow, crows and more crows. She gave us a hard time in class because she wouldn't write things down, she let them spill out on stage. We had to follow her thinking without knowing what she was thinking and all the time thinking we weren't really seeing what we thought we were seeing.

Steven painted a couch. Not just whitewash but really painted a picture on the couch. I think that show was called "Fish Head Soup." I tried my hand at carving and jewellery making. I liked the watercolour work more than oil painting. There wasn't any space to use the oils in class so I did those at my apartment. I was part of the art show in the Okanagan gallery with the students and staff and had some work in a few other shows. My art piece *Self Portrait* turned out to be the cover for my book and the first piece of art that I sold. At the end of my final year I sold a few more pieces. One set of three watercolours were sold to, I believe, the Osoyoos Band in the Okanagan.

There were many adventures to go on while at En'owkin. I attended a couple of book launches and while at a filming of a show for Vision TV with Dorothy Christian, found what it was like to have an obsession that turns into a piece of art.

We were filming for the launch of *In Honour of our Grandmothers*. I saw an art piece by George Littlechild. That picture kept going around in my mind, so much that it woke me up in the middle of the night. I had to get out of bed to jot down the words "Never Again" which became a poem in my book. I wrote that for George Littlechild.

I watched people come and go like the leaves on water. Some left never to return to the En'owkin. Some returned acting different. Aaron left, came back for a visit but didn't stay. It wasn't for him, I guess. Whenever you went to the office there was someone new to meet or greet. That was the beauty of the En'owkin, no one was a stranger. We were always having a potluck for some reason or other. When someone new came into town or an alumni returned for a visit we had another potluck.

Donna Goodleaf, the non-fiction teacher while I was at the En'owkin, was a blast. I had so much fun with her. We had serious conversations and yet, there was this elfish/pixyish type of spirit within her that seemed to bubble out infectiously. I'd feel like a kid again. She taught me about feminism. I'd never thought about it at all because of the Haudenosaunee matrilineal thought and philosophy. We never needed to fight for equality in the old days. She wrote great poems about her mom and the other women in her community and had a wonderful way of reading those poems that made you want to go and visit her mom. Being a Mohawk from Kanawake she knew many of the people I knew or knew of them. She also knew about bologna and potato chip sandwiches. I often wonder where she went.

Donna was the maid of honour when two En'owkin Teachers, Beth and Gerry, got married. We had three Mohawk women do a performance piece at their ceremony (actually, we read a poem). The students decorated our little hall and the community helped with food. It was a family affair. We had fun and boy, did I get tired. I kept forgetting that I was older than some of the teachers and I was definitely older than the students. But I was a student and to me that meant I could do what they did... *almost.*

One of the things that I learned about in my past years (not only at En'owkin) was the connection between creativity, sexuality and spirituality. Those into chakras will know this area. Working in close proximity with artists and writers gave us the energy to create. It is a spiritual connection and it sometimes worked into a sexual connection. When I arrived, a couple of the girls were already pregnant. When I left, a few more were pregnant. That is not a bad thing. The spirituality, creativity, and the sexuality were working together. When I look back at my days at En'owkin I can say that I birthed a book while others birthed babies.

I came away from the school with many wonderful memories. I felt like a family member within Jeannette's family. I felt like a community member in Penticton, both on the reserve and off. I protested the destruction of the natural hunting grounds and helped blockade the road. I learned that night, standing in the freezing cold, that it is better to protest with pen and paper. I went picking berries and ate traditional foods at ceremonies. I went to funerals and birthday parties. I travelled to some wonderful places and met many wonderful people. I had my first experience at a casino in the state of Washington and learned after a roll of nickels that I don't like casinos. I actually knew that before but went to be polite because after that we went for Mexican food, another passion of mine.

All the beauty, family and adventure aside, I also became the nerd of the school and constantly did my homework. I walked to school carring many books. I read a lot and did what I was instructed. I enjoyed the artistic experience and found ways of expressing myself besides my writing. I also learned why most artists are so critical of their work. Perception. I saw beauty in the work of a student named Cheryl who kept telling me the work wasn't good enough. I now know what that means since I started to create and show more of my own art.

As I sit here in my home working on art pieces and writing pieces I have fond memories of school. Getting a Masters Degree in American Studies at the University of Buffalo was fun and interesting but nowhere near my experience at En'owkin.

I went to visit the En'owkin school in 1999. It has changed not, only location but, structurally as well. The dream of Jeannette and her community members has evolved into reality. The school is now in their home community, not in the little town. The people are still there, warm and friendly, to welcome you when you go in the door.

I want to go back. Not to stay but to have a reunion, to touch base with the men and women and see where we are and where we have come from. I'm at Six Nations being part of the Six Nations Writers. I have my own publishing business now *Shaking the Rattle* will be back in print. I'm an artist and getting ready for a show with three other women in November. Many wonderful things have gone on in my life since graduating. I've learned so much with the tools I received from En'owkin. I've emerged from student to writer and artist. For that I must thank all the students and teachers that were part of my life for two wonderful years from 1994 to 1996.

En'owkin

family away
from home
is En'owkin
centered in creativity
spirituality and culture

with a pen in my hand
I went there
with a desire
to learn
to write

and I did learn
to live breathe
indigenous rhythm

living in the Okanagan
was an honor
I respect and love
my En'owkin family

Raven's Take on the Okanagan

The Okanagan,
Raven says
she's hot.
Gorgeous valleys,
sensual and serene.
Beautiful lakes
with waves
calm inspiring
or strong determined.
Sage graces
the earth.

You'll have to excuse Raven,
he is rather ambiguous
about whether he referred
to the Okanagan landscape
or Okanagan women.

For his defense,
he says
the Okanagan women,
they are beautiful
because their land is beautiful.

Raven loves the Okanagan

Community

with our hands open
we bring cedar to the flame
singing praying learning
community is an ancient rhythm

Reunite

Together they gathered, reuniting for the first time since the original time they had all come together. In the forest, they gathered and memories resurfaced. In the open gathering space in the forest the sun shone on the soft, wild grass and budding spring sunflowers.

Beaver was there first, eagerly awaiting everyone's arrival. He paced in a circle dragging his heavy tail on the ground, flattening the grass to make a spot for everyone to dance.

Magpie flew in and noisily started chattering. "I knew you'd be the first one here, Beaver. I'm going to look around and come back when things get more exciting." She flew off squawking and muttering to herself.

Chipmunk arrived and tiptoed across the flattened grass toward Beaver to touch noses with him. "I don't want to mess your lovely pattern," Chipmunk gently squeaked.

"So good to see you old friend," laughed Beaver, "It has been a long time."

Branches began snapping and breaking to the left of the circle.

"Tansi. Long time," barreled a voice through the dense forest.

Beaver and Chipmunk turned toward the voice. It was *Wesakechak.* Just as he was about to enter the circle, *Wesakechak* was startled from behind as a sneaky coyote jumped at his heels.

"Ha-ha, silly one. I've been following you for days and you didn't even sense me. Ha-ha, he-he..."

Coyote rolled on the ground in laughter. *Wesakechak* frowned as Beaver and Chipmunk laughed with Coyote.

"Wait until *Napi* gets here, you'll get paybacks." *Wesakechak* said scornfully.

He paused then broke into laughter too. He was patting his old friend Coyote on the back when a deer nervously poked her head through the trees. There was a fawn with her, who tried to hide behind her legs but bravely peered out.

"Look," cried Beaver, "Deer had her baby. She is beautiful."

They all looked over and the fawn hid behind Deer's legs.

"Awww, ever cute," said Coyote.

Everyone agreed with sounds of "Mmm-hhhm" and nodded their heads.

A large Buck marched out which Deer and Fawn followed into the circle.

Soon everyone began to arrive. From the East, North, South and West, everyone came together. *Nanabush* from the East, Salmon, Buffalo, Two Spirits, Wolf, Quail, Raven, Gramma *Kookum* Moon, Sister Stars, Roots and Berries, Swan, Whale, Frog with her tadpoles, Magpie, Spider, Owl, Bear, Snake, Corn Woman, Beetle, Grouse, *Nauq* from the North, Walrus, Wolverine, Shamans, Eagle, Mountain Lion, *Wesakechak* and many others. The visiting began. West Coast Raven sat with cousin Prairie Crow. Sturgeon, who had grown to a glorious size, told Okanagan Lake that he was thinking of making her his home. They had returned to the original place where they had all met – En'owkin.

The earth shook as Grizzly Bear stood high on her hind legs and began to speak. Everyone hushed except Coyote who was still snickering and teasing *Wesakechak*. Grizzly Bear hunched down to stare Coyote right in the eyes. Coyote's fur ruffled in the hot air blowing from Bear's huge nostrils. Coyote shrugged his head between his shoulders with his ears drawn back and his tail curled between his legs. Bear stood again.

"How wonderful to have everyone together again." She raised her arms to the sky. "I remember when we were all together the first time. I learned much from every one of you. You all shared your knowledge and insight. And now we are reunited."

"Mmm-hhhm," There were many murmurs of agreement. Bear finished his speach and other spoke and reminised of their shared time together at En'owkin.

Later *Wesakechak* made a large fire and began to tell stories. Prairie Grouse danced while Moon drummed a Spirit Song. Darkness filled the night sky and the fire glowed with great intensity. Coyote walked toward the outhouse, continually looking back over his shoulder into the darkness. A twig snapped under his paw and he sprug like a spring into the air. He went into a fast trot with his tail between his legs. He didn't see *Napi* and *Wesackechak* sneaking through the woods behind him.

When *Napi* and *Wesackechak* reached the outhouse door they could barely contain their laughter. They flung the door open and howled in voices so loud that the treetops quivered. Coyote yipped and sprung into the air with his eyes rolled back in his head. He fell down the hole in the outhouse. Splash. "Gross!" yelled Coyote from within the hole. "Help! Get me out of here!" He hollered and squealed. *Napi* and *Weesackecha* laughed and tossed a rope down the hole.

Magpie heard all the commotion and came flying to see what had happened. *Napi* and *Weesackecha* were holding their bellies, laughing and rolling on the ground. Magpie laughed too. She nattered, "Now you two are going to be sorry. You all should just stop. This is going to go on and on and someone is going to end up with hurt feelings or worse. And don't be getting me involved in this nonsense. I can just see it now... one of these times..." On and on Magpie nattered until no one listened at all.

Coyote spent an hour in the creek, gagging and sneezing and continually dunking himself in the water. He got out and shook himself over and over until he was dizzy but almost dry. He held his head high with his nose up in the air as he walked back into the Gathering circle. He stood in the center of the circle and announced to everyone that when he fell in the outhouse he wasn't scared and that he did it intentionally to make his fur shiny.

"Mmmm-hhmm," everyone nodded as though they agreed, but chuckles were still heard amongst the crowd.

Magpie squawked and complained about the smell. Coyote kept interrupting as she squawked until she finally got so fed up that she flew to the other side of the gathering where she continued to complain.

The Elders said a prayer that made everyone's hearts and spirits so full they all began to float; even big Sturgeon and Walrus floated in the night sky.

"This is beautiful," said Grizzly Bear, "Look at what we all can do when we put out spirit creative energy together."

Frog blew bubbles out of her mouth that floated up into the atmosphere. Being afraid of heights, Coyote held his eyes shut tightly.

The fire's glow reached all the way to the treetops where everyone floated and glided. The night sky glowed with a grey luminescence that cast a silver shadow upon their furs, scales, skins and feathers. After a time, they floated back to the gathering circle. Everyone joined hands then drummed and sang the Okanagan Honor Song. More stories were shared that night.

Wesakechak told the story of an adventure with Two Spirit and how they got stuck on the side of a mountain and became covered in cactus needles. Goose spoke of Blue Bird's song which was so beautiful, that all he could do was sit and weep while she sang.

In reuniting they realized that although they were still the same, they had also changed. They had grown, transformed and developed into more enlightened beings. They had expanded original knowledge by sharing it with one another.

A place they all came to – En'owkin. Some came to find healing, some came to create, some didn't know why they came until they arrived. With mountains to the East and West and lakes to the North and South, the valley cradled them in safety like a mother holding a baby. Many left, some stayed. Sturgeon stayed deep in the darkness depths of Okanagan Lake. And today, people tell stories of a great creature in the lake.

Caught in Fear

There's this certain crow, a game-boy rider he calls himself. Small spotted eagle sees him tailing among the others, and before she knows it, he's on her back, literally, holding on for his life. Turns out he's afraid of heights, though he only admits this in so many words. What he says is, crow at one time was pure white, with the sweetest singing voice of all the birds. Like many others, he volunteers to steal fire from the people who live east of grandmother moon, but, being a perfectionist, he takes so long hovering over the fire – trying to find the perfect piece to steal – his white feathers smoke to black. When he returns to his village he tries to sing the first rap tune, but he'd inhaled so much smoke that out comes a raw, caw, caw, and his flight pattern's been off ever since.

Now this in-crowd crow says a basket was left at the side of the road for the woman, and since he gave his maw-caws his word in return for breakfast in bed all next week, he'd like to keep his distance. She'll need what's in there, thinks the crow, so small spotted eagle agrees to set down the basket next to the lodge. She is here to gift a story, that small spotted eagle tells him, and she asks this crazy crow could he unhook himself from her back now and leave her feathers he's toe-combed from her back, leave them in the basket for the woman, she'll need those too, stay and play awhile, hey?, and so goes this story.

it is said that once
long time ago
two extraordinary young women
after dreams of future days
of prayer songs
of medicine ways
and loving only women
refuse marriage
to any man

after many years
while still young

the two women meet and grow
in power
in strength
in love

while most young men
respect the gifted ones
who see as true women
who see as true men
there are two young men who
fancy themselves to be
alluring appealing charming
tempting interesting fascinating
attracting captivating
beyond splendor
and follow the women
in secret

so that even after the elders tell them
no
let these women be
the men persist
and in time are forbidden
even
to speak
to be
in their company

then one fine summer day
all hush and hush
far into the woods
where the women peel
and collect tree bark
and bathe themselves nearby
the men follow

in the water the women
express their love

their passions sweet
and the men are witness to this
moment movement mystery time
when one of the women
the older one

transforms but half her beauty
into the needle of a pine
and that half
floats on the water
to the mouth of her companion
the younger one
who swallows
and soon after becomes
big with child
a green-eyed child whose name
soft-shell turtle woman
remains in song

and so it is said
that from the water
they obtained
their spirit power

And so it is said, too, not too long ago, when the forests are still strong, city doctors kill a medicine woman, calling her a witch, because they are in a jealous rage after she heals a woman they aren't able to heal. She is so powerful, she uses only water, bathes and prays for the woman for four days and brings her back to full health. This is how this story is told to small spotted eagle by her grandmother, who is told by her grandmother, who is told by her grandmother is how small spotted eagle is told in her language.

Quarter Indian

8:56 p.m. Friday.
I don't want you to get worried but I've packed up Princess and her stuff and we've checked into a hotel. Luckily, she's asleep. Certain people are saying I'm a narcotics officer and a rat. I don't need to put up with that. We're just gonna lay low for the night. We've got full cable, so we'll just watch t.v.

I still haven't slept. I partied my ass off last night with a hottie from Burnaby. We gotta get this office shit done so I can rest. How come you never told me there were so many good lookin Indians at your work? Man, I just gotta get some sleep. Are we going for lunch first?

12:56 a.m. Saturday.
I'm a police officer with the Sardis RCMP. I'm at the hospital with your daughter and ex-husband. It seems as though he's suffering from some sort of psychotic episode involving paranoid delusions and voices. Does he have a history of drug use? If you give me directions to your house, I'll try to get authorization to drive her home. I'll call you back.

Give me the business information that has to be sorted out, then you can get started on the tax forms. I'll separate any tax papers so you'll have something to work with. Was this CD in with the pile of papers? I wonder what's on it? I'll check it in case there are past tax forms or business files from previous years.

2:10 a.m. Saturday:
Sorry to disturb you at this hour. I'm the after-hours clerk for the provincial Ministry of Children and Families. Do you have any relatives in the area that could come and pick-up your daughter? If not, we might try to acquire taxi service for you. I will call you right back.

Oh, it's just porn. It looks like some of this is late seventies, early eighties. Head bands and leg warmers. Nothing worse than outdated porn. I gotta change the format just to see files, I don't need a slide show. Not all of it's porn though. Hey, there are movies on this disc too.

I'm never gonna get any sleep, am I?

2:35 a.m. Saturday:
Hello again. I'm just calling to let you know that we've contacted a taxi company and they're sending one for you now. You'll be driven to the Sardis police station to pick up your daughter. The ministry will cover the bill.

Some of these are personal photos. Like that one. Isn't that your friends kid? Why would there be personal photos with old *porn*? Let's see what's on those movies. Wait a minute... those are kids! Oh, sick man. Some of this is kiddie porn. Didn't that girl used to live in your complex?

3:05 a.m. Saturday.
Hey. Are you almost here? I was wondering if you could do me a favor. I don't really feel safe here in Sardis because of those people. Can I get a lift with you in the taxi? Maybe stay with you for a couple of days until I can get a new place. Or can you drive me to my friend's place in New West? I can't stay here. Think about it and let me know. I'm so glad you could get here.

We weren't really sure what to do with this. I was looking for business files and came across the pictures. Sure enough, these ones are pretty gross. There's this woman... but look there. That's her daughter! We know that guy in the picture. When she was five, he must have been in his mid-thirties.

3:30 a.m. Saturday.
Hello. I'm the officer you spoke with earlier. Your daughter seems to be fine. She has not been harmed in any way but I don't think she's had dinner. Although your ex-husband feels like he's in serious danger, we don't perceive any immediate threat to himself or others. Here are your daughters bags. We escorted them back to the hotel to claim their things. We're glad you have your daughter back.

Can you believe this! I'm in a North Vancouver RCMP detachment waiting to give my statement and my ex calls. Says he's being called names. Of all the nerve. He checked himself and my kid into a hotel to hide out. He just doesn't get it. He's a parent too. He has responsibilities equal to mine. He's wimping out. He'll try and send her back early by getting sick or something. I told him, "Too bad. Deal with it."

4:10 a.m. Saturday.
Yeah. I just thought I'd leave a message. I got Punkin back. The cabbie bought me a coffee at Timmy's. No I haven't been to sleep yet. It's been 45 hours. I'll call you when I wake up. Punkin hasn't slept either, I'm sure she'll sleep in. We're driving along the Trans-Canada highway from Sardis to Surrey in a taxi paid for by the Ministry of Children and Families shortly after four a.m. on a Saturday. I'm drinking a coffee paid for by a sympathetic cabbie, looking at the daughter I rescued from my ex-husband and his self-centred, irresponsible lifestyle. All this following finding evidence and giving a statement in connection with violations against kids.

Punkin looks up at me and asks, "Mom. Am I a quarter Indian?"

"Yes, baby you sure are," I replied.

"So when I grow up am I gonna be a toonie Indian?"

> Facilitator David Rattray opened an education conference workshop with one simple statement: "We cannot heal our society until we stop treating our children like sexual pincushions."

3:00 p.m. Tuesday.
A constable in the Sex Crimes Unit called and informed me that the RCMP have not filed charges. They interviewed the young girl, who told the officers that she wasn't in the photos. After interviewing the mother and the suspect, they have determined the only charge they're investigating is possession of child pornography. Dismayed, I say, "Well, if that wasn't her, then who? We know that's him. My neighbor lived with the suspect in the apartment depicted in those photos. She bought him the blanket they're lying on and that's even her sewing machine in the background." The constable seems caught off-guard by that response. She admitted that she didn't know about the personal photos having thought they were all downloaded off the internet. She also confessed to not having read our statements. She had based the interview questions solely on the overview of the initial investigating

officer!

My neighbor went to the police station equipped with personal pictures supporting the identification of the people and places on the disc. The investigation continues to probe into the contents of the CD. My neighbor is going on holidays soon and hopefully will be able to get on with her life. I'll be staying home with my daughter watching helplessly as she plays hoping I can save her from the pain I saw in the eyes of those violated children, disappointed that my struggle is hampered by her father's poor personal choices. I will tell her stories of quarters, toonies and Indians.

Spring Songs, Summer Memories

I can still hear her feathery voice
echoing
tiny whispers.
Silky words threading
and
weaving extrusive threads
Brushing my heart.
Delicately whisking buttery hair.
"Wheest, wheest, wheest."
Nut-brown eyes soft and glittery
"Do you want me to *chooch* you too?"
Green giddy eyes! "You gotta choose me too!"
Whistling songbird scooping us up
Note by note
Twin eyes gleaming
Illuminating the dusty kitchen.
Baby bugs
hopping
on the floor.
Bright pretty red polka dot bandana
Wrapped delicately around her head
Sweaty hands
Yellow wooden handled straw broom.
Tiny puffs of dust
dancing on the wooden floor.
exquisite chirping spring chickadee.
Spoons banging on the floor
"un hun a way ho. un hun a way ho!"
Tiny lungs
bolting out verses...

GETTING dizzy!

Stick-game melody
So graceful
At what seemed an eternity

Home Drum Beat

Mother's humanitarian rythmn
calls to us
drawing us back
where the land meets the soul
and we have metaphysical understanding

Grandmother Stories

One day I will tell all of the stories but not yet. I can feel them wriggling around under the blanket of my skin, like children. They are waiting to be tamed but at the moment they are wild and free, and that is part of the reason I don't like to say too much about them, because I remember those days when I was also wild and free.

If you look around you, you will see that many people are like that, and say very little, even though they are always watching. All the watchers know who each other is. There are a couple of societies like that – the watchers and the non-watchers, who are often the loud talkers and the exhibitionists. We don't mind who they are. Quite often, we are forced to mix, but on the other hand, we naturally gravitate into one of the two societies. My understanding of these things is very old.

It's true that some of us old ones look around for young ones who can fill our boots. We might not say anything, but to ourselves we will say, "Oh, there's a good one. He looks like he'll be able to make it," and then we'll be sure to let that young one know we're keeping our eyes on him and we are proud of him. So automatically at a very young age, even as young as 3 years old, he will already begin to be alert about what he's doing and how he's doing it.

The watching society is the mysterious one. We never talk about it, but we make secret plans to meet each other. Sometimes it's only to stand in a doorway and see the other one across the room. My own father did this to me many times. It's just to give evidence that we are conscious about them. Of course, they can retaliate, but normally the silence is not broken. We know what's going on when suddenly, perhaps when getting food from the table for instance, suddenly we are in the same line-up, and one of us ladles some food onto the other's dish. Or we smile and say something like, "Oh, you forgot your purse," or whatever. So it is little things like that which are the way we 'prove' that our watching is shared.

I was going to say also, these people never brag about what they do, even if they do it very well. Usually you never hear them do that. Someone will say, "Oh, I heard you made such-and-such an achievement" and it will be at those times that we answer something like, "Well, it was just an accident that I had the time to get it done." The meaning is that we do not wish to pay attention to things like that because they are already in the past, and to speak further about these things is a minor irritation. For instance, someone will go out and be very successful at hunting and feed a lot of people but at the same time, you will never know when he did this, but you find he has already done it. Then the people say, "Oh, whose meat is this I am eating?"

"Oh, it's from the Edgar's (family)" and that's about all you will know, because if you want to find out about how he did that, you'll just have to hang around with him for awhile and spend some time with him.

I was given a gift sometime when I was a young woman. My great-grandmother medicine woman appeared to me and told me her visions were jumping to me, meaning that they skipped a generation, maybe because my father was married to a French woman. Anyhow it was like something poured down my throat, so I can feel that water in my body acting up every-once-in-awhile. I had a strange woman's attitude to things which I suppose one could call individualistic, that is, my ideas didn't come from anywhere else, and the ones that did, mostly seemed to bounce off me. Many times in my life I wondered where I got my ideas about who I was, from, or about what marriage and a good husband was, about what babies were feeling, and things like that.

It was as though I never had to ask anyone what was going on, or I always felt silly when I did, as though I would know those answers if I just kept quiet instead. So a lot of my life was experimental and a weaving in and out of realities of all kinds which people spoke about, although I never had much to do with any of those realities.

Beliefs to me were something transitory, not because they were for other people, but because for me I only felt interested in them for a little while at a time. At first I thought this was some kind of flaw in myself, but eventually I could see that it wasn't, because there was a better way of looking at the things, which I was ignoring. The way things were, just so often seemed a result of time and place, even if the weight of the belief was centuries old. Most of my life I spent listening to everyone else and what mattered to them. I always felt comfortable doing this. I had things to say but that could wait. Now that I am older, I begin to feel responsible to share what I think. But I might not be old enough yet, so it's better to keep some of those 'half-baked' ideas to myself. In some way, we are never old enough to do anything, but this does not exempt us from being responsible.

Well, what that grandmother gave me was shocking and I can still taste the shock. I have gotten over not being attached to beliefs, but not quite sure I have gotten over what she gave me. Sometimes I think she's still alive, but I never met her or heard her voice. I think this when those visions she gave me wake up, stretch, and yawn. They do this when I see a piece of them outside myself, sometimes in someone's eyes, for instance. Usually they don't know they are reminding me of some visions I have had. Something wriggles out of their eyes and escapes very quickly, and a shadow passes over my eyes, and even though I pretend I have not seen anything, I have learned not to ignore these flashes of insight into their ancestors' worlds.

Other times, something happens in the way they move. The limbs make an arc, which freeze-frames itself in my mind, and it is in that instance that I "know" who they are, inside. Mostly I live with the insides of people but I have gotten used to the fact that most people don't do things that way. Rarely. So then when they ask something like, "So did you think what I said to those people was alright?" I'll answer, "Of course it was," because I know that all those words don't have much to do with what's really going on.

Eagle Feather Song

yesterday two eagle feathers came to me
I am white and I am red
I can sing of those things
no one taught
from the quiet, their voices still reach me

I am not male or female
I am white and red

in the old days in woodlands
running above the ground
brings everything from the past
into the present

when the feathers came to me
I heard the spirits sing again

let others speak of native peoples
yet hear no voices like these
I am white and I am red

when the line of our ancestors
is stretched
the white shears away
like tufts on a thistle
before I sip that power

I am red
for no reason the landscape
opens up and reveals
long ago times and rivers of song.

mother sings of the young men
whose hearts sang like birds
in their chests

mother sings of the young women
whose feet were so swift

mother sings of the elders
who brought you this song,
of the history
which brought you here

carry these feathers
for your grandfathers, grandmothers
and all your relations

before these hills and rivers sprang
tell them we knew where to live
and who we were
and how it was
in our woodland homes

tell them you know where to live
and who you are
and how it is
in your eagle homes

Testimony: Grandma

this is what an old man who drinks and smokes his entire life smells like, grandma
this is what old men must smell like before they die, grandma,
almost all the same, probably,
this is how they walk when they are old grandma,
I know you wondered about those things, they were all a mystery,
I know you wished your own mother could have lived as long as you,
I know you wondered why and how you lived so long,

this is what they do when they are angry, grandma,
they throw fits and talk venomously,
they yank the intravenous tubes out and attempt
to run out the hospital doors, they don't want to die amongst strangers
they want to be where you are grandma, smelling of roses,
where your fingers still embroider.

this is what an old man whose brothers were lost in the war drums like, grandma,
he comes and goes as he pleases and his children fight against his savagery,
into her old age your daughter loses the memory of all the painful years,
she forgets the name of her first-born, grandma
and his only son vanishes before our eyes, at the bottom of the stairs,
in front of the widow with the widow's chin,
remarrying two more men like him who die before their time,

his other daughter, nipped in the bud at six months, you mourned
her sweet watery eyes your whole life, grandma,
with every silken stitch of doll's clothes you made for her -
so many dolls, they spilled overtop the upright glass display case,
your grandchildren's fingers eagerly smudged, swooning over
brightly colored ribbons

this is what an old man who spent seventy-five blustery northern
Canadian winters looks like, grandma,
walking the ties, checking the brakes, with breath like dragon-smoke
frozen over an icy sea of crystals,
face and hands of tanned red leather, unlike the hands of your own
saintly father and mother
arching gracefully round your thin shoulders, holy born

holy born woman I have lived so long your bones have turned to
dust, grandma,
in my dreams I seek the final resting place no one dared to touch, I
watched them run away,
your only one, curious ears straining
heard your body rustle in its shroud one last time beside the pew,
even the chubby priest could not linger so long in your radiance,
the embalmer's eyes, still watering like your lost one's eyes,
lingering with grief over your unimpeachable grace, drowned in
ceremony, aghast
and wandering like a ghost amongst strangers,
your son-in-law's silence a river of testimony
to every steaming glass of tea you ever made,
his shadow today, a testimony to the indelible fabric you were woven
of, grandma

Grand Entry

"Oh…my....God. What the hell is he doing here?" Sherry said more to herself than to Karen who was sitting beside her at the top of a small baseball bleacher.

"Who? Who?" Karen asked while she chewed a mouthful of bannock.

"His Royal Highness, Wannabe Chief Premier Poops-A-Lot. Shhh. Don't look and don't turn around. He's right behind us. Just wait till he walks by."

Karen chewed slowly so she wouldn't choke and miss finding out who this illustrious person was. "Okay, look to your left but don't make it obvious. There, in the black leather jacket," Sherry indicated by pointing her lips.

"What, Who? I don't know who? Is it Elvis?"

"No. It's Todd Brown."

"Who?"

"Todd Brown. He's the head of the Urban Aboriginal Coalition. He wants to be head honcho of everything. Him and his little band of cronies."

"Ahhh," Karen said, not really caring.

"It's gotta be an election somewhere because I've never seen him at a pow-wow," Sherry continued. "And if I see him kissing papooses I'm going to upchuck my bannock."

"Gee, Sherry. We're at a pow-wow. You shouldn't be talking bad about other people at a pow-wow."

"Yeah well he shouldn't be doing bad anywhere. He's just a power-hungry self-centred unqualified idiot."

"Holuh, Sherry. You better go to a meeting or a sweat."

"He's the one who should be sweating. He plays dirty politics and if his nose were any browner you'd say it was a piece of poo."

Karen rolled her eyes as the announcer spoke.

"Okay people, five minutes to grand entry!"

Soon, the line up of dancers and dignitaries at the east entrance of the pow-wow arena were ready. Small baseball bleachers and lawn chairs of various types for the dancers and their families formed a circle. In front of the announcer stand sat the Host Drum of eight men sitting around a big drum. To the right were eight more drum groups lined up. Another group had just arrived and were setting up. Anticipation was thick in the early evening air. The whipman in the center of the circle gave one last look around then waved a stick in a small circle in the air.

The announcer spoke, "Hokah! Everyone please rise. It's pow-wow time! Grand entry time!"

The host drum started the grand entry song. People stood up and the flag and staff carriers danced into the circle. They were followed by a few Native Veterans and then the head woman and man dancers. Then the order of dancers from Golden Age men, Golden Age women, men's traditional, women's traditional and on, down to the tiny tots. Karen was smiling and enjoying the procession of bright colors, magnificent creative outfits of beads, shiny jingles and feathers.

Sherry, looking at each dancer's regalia, liked watching the graceful movements of the dancers and how they proudly danced in time to the beat of the drum, the heart beat of Mother Earth. She didn't know why but when the tiny tots danced in she felt like crying. She tried to hide her tears by looking down and fiddling with her purse. Maybe it was the beat of the drums or the song that was coming through the speakers or the beauty of a sky slowly fading to darker shades of blue or maybe her period was coming but, she saw the beauty of her people despite all the crap they had to go through. Here they were in this one moment in time all beautiful. Sherry tried to memorize this picture forever.

Once the last tiny tot dancer was in, the grand entry song ended. The dancers stood in a circle as the flag and victory song were sung. Everyone remained standing as an elder from the reserve gave a prayer in his language, then English. After the opening words of welcome, the announcer introduced the many princesses from other pow-wows. That's when Karen and Sherry took off to the porta-potties. It was embarrassing to come out of a porta-potty and there was some handsome traditional dancer waiting in line. So they always made sure to go while the dancers were still on the floor.

"Let's go get something to eat now," Karen suggested.

"Sure."

While standing in the line Sherry noticed that Todd Brown was a couple of people behind her. She felt herself blush and was glad that her long auburn hair hid her burning ears. She was still angry with him because she wasn't short-listed for a job interview. He hired a woman that he was romantically involved with. Sherry went to school with her. The woman always put her hand up in class and would go off on a tangent about her life and getting mad at other students if they interrupted. When Sherry and other students expressed concern to the professor, he said, "When you go out in the real world you will have to deal with people like that. Learn to deal with it here." Sherry had taken out a student loan for three thousand dollars and didn't want to hear this woman's life story every damned class. She was sure that this woman would never get a job in the real world.

"Sherry!"

"What?"

"You're next."

Sherry looked at the young girls working the concession who were waiting for her to order. "Oh sorry. One salmon dinner and a Pepsi, please." She turned to Karen and said, "Yep, there's nothing better in the whole world than some barbecued salmon and an ice cold Pepsi."

They got their plates and turned around. Sherry was glad Todd was looking at the menu board and not at her. She wasn't sure if he even remembered who she was.

"I just can't stand that guy," Sherry said as they walked back to their seats.

"Who?"

"Todd Brown Noser."

"Oh cripes, Sherry. Forget about it! Are you still mad that you didn't get the job?"

"Yes and because he hired an airhead who is not qualified for the job. It's not who you know, it's who you blow. You know, I used to respect him but now I've heard too much crap about him. I'm beginning to believe it's true. I don't care what AA says. Everyone talks about other people anyway. Look at old Doris, always talking shit about me. Saying I try to snag her boyfriends. Have you seen her boyfriends? Yikes. That jealous old hag."

"Are you sure you're not jealous?"

"Jealous? Jealous of what? That we have to suffer because if you're not part of some stupid little clique you can't get hired anywhere? It's the people that suffer because these pot smoking Indian yuppies who want power don't know anything about anything? Where are the real leaders? Where's the humbleness and humility? There's no real Indians anymore."

"Wow. I didn't realize that. You mean there's no real Indians here?" Karen asked.

"I don't know. This seems so commercialized. Oh great. Look. There's Kirsten. If there's any name I hate more in the world it's Kirsten. Look at her fake Indian jacket, fringe and all. Is that a real Indian?"

"Sherry. You're wearing an Indian Motorcycle t-shirt."

"Yeah. Well that's different. I'm cool."

"Hey, you know why they have fringe on those jackets?" Karen piped up.

"I don't know. To look pretty?"

"No, the water falls off it there, instead of getting the coat all soaked."

"Wow. I didn't know that." Sherry imagined rain falling off the fringe.

Todd made up his mind and was ready to order. "Three Indian tacos, one coffee and two apple juices. Do you have a box I can use to carry everything?" He wished he had his two sons with him to carry the stuff but he had wanted them to save their place on the top bleachers.

"Why do we have to come here Dad? This is weird," said Cameron his twelve year old when they'd pulled up to the pow-wow parking lot.

"It's not weird. I want my boys to experience all cultures. I want you guys to listen to all kinds of music and see all kinds of art."

"How long do we have to stay here?" Asked ten year old Brandon.

"Not too long. I just need to talk to some people and then we'll go."

Todd was impressed with the grand entry. He wondered if there would be a chance to mention the upcoming election to the crowd and wished he had spoken to the organizers about it before hand. Todd prided himself on his public speaking skills. Joining Toastmasters was the best thing he had done for his career. This election was a stepping stone, he had it all planned out. That picture on the front page of them with the Premier was a coup, an image that would be subconsciously planted in people's heads: a First Nation in Parliament. It was weird but he admired Hitler because of the way he could work a crowd. Todd could also work a crowd. He felt that most Native people knew nothing about politics, he would be the one to lead them out of the dark ages. When he got back to their seats, the boys were gone. He spotted them at a toy stand and went over.

"Can we have money, Dad?" asked Brandon.

"Not now, later. Look our seats are gone now damn it. We have to find other seats. Come on."

They walked around outside the arbor and Todd looked up at the bleachers. There weren't any empty seats near the announcer stand. He cursed silently. Todd knew where to be noticed. Walking around is good too, he thought. He saw many people he knew and said hello. They were mostly West Coast artisans with booths. Finally he spied a space on the first tier of the bleachers. He directed his sons to sit and sat between them. He passed them their food and then put on his sunglasses and started to eat. "Mmmm. Good tacos."

"Man, does the Great Spirit have a sense of humor or what? Bonehead is sitting directly across from us." Sherry informed Karen.

"We came here to enjoy the pow-wow not beat on boneheads. Just get over it and move on with your life. People might think you have a crush on him or something."

"Don't be retarded."

"Hey, I remember that you said he was good looking before."

"Yeah, that was before I knew what an a-hole he was."

"You're jealous."

"I am not."

Sherry decided to ignore Todd and to not make any more comments about him. She savored every bite of the warm salmon.

"I'm stuffed. We have to dance off this supper. I hope they have an intertribal soon. Will you dance, Sherry? Maybe during the Owl Dance you can ask Todd to dance."

Sherry ignored her and watched the dancers going around in a colorful human merry-go-round. They both stood when the Golden age categories danced. Sherry was annoyed that Todd and his sons remained sitting. "No respect," she muttered. The women watched the men's category keenly. Sherry tried to make eye contact with one dancer but felt stupid later when she saw him sitting beside a pretty lady in a women's traditional outfit. *I'm worlds away from these pow-wow people; a city girl.* She looked into the distance at Mount Baker and could see it's white top in the fading light. *Maybe some day I'll dance pow-wow. I belong to AA right now and I dance to the beat of a different drum. Techno.* Sherry smiled to herself then stopped suddenly. She had to find a job soon.

She would graduate with a B.A. next month and it wasn't fair that Kirsten was flouncing around in a factory fringe jacket because she dropped out of school due to 'family problems'. Everyone knew she was just stupid! Sherry watched Kirsten push her big butt down beside a couple on the bleachers where Todd sat. When Kirsten leaned over her cleavage showed. *Has she no shame?*

It was getting chilly as the September sun set. Sherry put on her black hoody and zipped it up. She saw Kirsten leave her seat and walk towards the porta-potties. Sherry stood and told Karen she was going to the washroom.

"Want me to come?"

"Naw. It's okay."

Sherry timed it just right. She saw Kirsten go into a porta-potty and she waited. She didn't know why but she wanted to tell Kirsten she was graduating. Kirsten came out and washed her hands by the porta-sinks. Sherry noticed her silver jewelry shining.

"Hi Kirsten."

Kirsten turned, "Oh hi Sharon."

Kirsten always called her Sharon and Sherry knew it was on purpose.

"It's Sherry. How's it going?"

"Everything's going great. You?"

"I'm going to graduate this spring."

"Good for you. I don't believe in the white man's school anymore. Who needs it? Sorry, I gotta run."

She left and Sherry watched her take a set of keys from her purse and, zap, the door of a new white truck open. Sherry went back to her seat.

Karen said, "They're going to have a 50/50 draw. Let's get tickets."

Sherry didn't want to tell Karen about Kirsten's truck. "Yeah, I'll buy some tickets when they come over this way." She saw Todd take off his leather jacket and stretch out two toned arms while a young girl measured a roll of tickets against them. People around him laughed. Some genius had come up with the marketing technique and it seemed to work. People were buying tickets like crazy. Karen and Sherry each bought one arm's length of tickets.

Sherry's mind wasn't on the pow-wow at all. She was pondering the unfairness of her situation and wondering how she could remedy it. She couldn't send a letter to the local Native newspaper because the editor/owner was Todd's friends. She could write an anonymous letter to the city telling them how incompetent he was, but that was her own opinion based on his hiring of an airhead. She'd heard he drank at a snazzy bar. Maybe she could go there with a camera and catch him.

The announcer said the next song was a Round Dance. "Everyone up, dancers and audience join in." There was already about fifty people out on the floor and more joining in.

Karen stood up, "Come on, Sherry."

"No way."

"Oh come on. It's dark now and it looks like fun."

It was dark and the electric motor run lights weren't much help. They were many people out on the floor now. Sherry didn't know the step but when she noticed that others didn't know it either she allowed Karen to pull her up. She was holding hands with Karen when another lady grabbed her other hand.

"Watch my feet!" Karen yelled as she side stepped to the double beat of the drum. Sherry soon caught on. It was fun. There must have been two hundred people in the circle. The people on her left turned in the other direction so as to shake hands with the people down the line. Sherry shuffled along and enjoyed shaking hands with people. There were male traditional dancers with their face painted, she couldn't tell if they were smiling, shy young people who didn't look at your face, old people that smiled kindly and beautiful women in their regalia. Some hands were cold and some were warm. Someone shook her hand hard and said hello in a familiar voice. It was Todd.

Sherry wasn't sure if he knew her but in that split second he spoke she saw something in his eyes that told her he was genuinely having fun. He seemed innocent and vulnerable. The next two hands belonged to his sons. Neither boy looked at her. The announcer asked more people to join in. Sherry didn't think there could be more people. They all held hands again.

Suddenly, everyone ran forward to the middle of the circle and cried “Whoooo!” They walked backwards holding hands and everyone danced around again. Sherry and Karen were laughing loud. The elder people left the circle and the young people ran forward again. When the dance was over, Sherry was out of breath. She climbed up the bleachers and took a long drink from a water bottle. People were dancing again. She saw Karen out there, but not Todd or his sons.

Karen came over. “It’s an intertribal. Come on,” she said extending her hand.

“I can’t.”

“Yes, you can. It’s easy. I’ll teach you. Come on, don’t be a wuss. It’s just toe, heel down, toe, heel down.”

Sherry laughed and let Karen pull her onto the dance floor.

In this World

In this World our two paths come together
We walk alone separate
We think different
You are a woman
I am a man
You and I fall in love with each other
We fall out of love and into love shock
There are a few brave and courageous women
There are a few brave and courageous men
There are sober and healthy people
Bravery is learning about themselves
A few will find themselves and love themselves
People hide behind their own face masks
People fear true happiness in themselves
People disconnect their heart from their head
Life is not about money or materialism or computers
Life is love energy earth energy
Life is giving knowledge away for free and not for money or gain
The world curtain has fallen shut
Our final act is being played out on a stage
A happy memory unfolds between two friends

In this world our two paths have come together.

Section 4

Rushing Water

Excerpt from *True Confession* Article

True Confessions of a German Indianthusiast, or How Things 'Just Happen'

[I] have often had to relate stories and explain the details of why I am interested in First Nations literatures to those Native students and colleagues I have had the pleasure to work with. They expected and demanded that I should come to them as a whole person, not just as a distant "participant observer" or supposedly "neutral scholar." While teaching at or networking with Native institutions and individuals I was encouraged to "think with the heart" not as an effort to suspend rational debate or scholarly research, but rather as an acknowledgement of the fact that, when dealing with people and their cultural productions, even in academia, we should allow our empathy to guide us. We should try never to forget the human ethics of our activities and remember that in order to survive well on this planet, respect and sharing are indispensable. But to "think with the heart" is an activity that can become very self defeating in Western academia where competition and jealousies easily lead to an attitude which slanders honesty as naivety, frankness as impertinence, openness as weakness, and suspects generosity as a tactical move. When I think with the heart in my normal university surroundings, competing colleagues are prone to misunderstand openheartedness as a weakness and use it for their own advancement.

In 1987, I visited Canada for the first time as the recipient of a Faculty Enrichment grant to conduct research for classes on Canadian women writers, on Canadian multiculturalism, and on Canadian regionalism, which allowed me to travel extensively. All the while, my mental antennae were out to simultaneously absorb information about Native people in Canada. Martin Heavyhead drove me around the Blood Reserve near Lethbridge, Alberta. Howard Adams showed Wolfgang Klooss and myself Metis sites around Prince Albert, Saskatchewan. Robin McGrath in London, Ontario provided me with information about Inuit authors. In Ottawa, Irenka Farmilo gave me the chance to see Tomson Highway's The Rez Sisters on stage, and through Parker Duchemin's seminar I met Wilfred Pelletier and Greg Young Ing. My non-Native research went quite well and all the people

I met were immensely helpful.

When I returned two years later on a Faculty Research grant things went in ways that were almost uncanny. My research focus was on Native literature, of which I had just taught a class back in Germany. This time, I brought a bibliography on index cards in a cardboard box, a camera, and a small tape recorder to interview writers, if possible. I also had with me four small eagle feathers which Ute Krause from Tokendorf in Schleswig-Holstein had given me to share. Prior to my departure, I had written to Theytus Books in Penticton, to Fifth House Publishers in Saskatoon and to Pemmican Press in Winnipeg, and had contacted some colleagues in advance. My hopes were high, and in my most daring dreams I thought of meeting writers whose works I had known for years and had always wanted to meet, like Maria Campbell, or "Bobbie Lee," or Jeannette Armstrong. My friend and comrade from Davis, the (now late) Howard Adams, had meanwhile returned to his Native Canada, and he set up a meeting for me with the then director of what later became the First Nations House of Learning at the University of British Columbia in Vancouver. That's where things began to fall into place. A series of things began to "just happen" which fell into a pattern far beyond my expectations.

While I checked their library holdings, Ethel B. Gardner at the Native Center at UBC was going through my cardboard box bibliography when all of a sudden she exclaimed, "Oh, Lee!" She'd come across my entry of the German translation of the book, Indian Rebel, written by a Canadian Indian women called Bobbie Lee whom I had never been able to locate under that name. Through Ethel I found out that Bobbie Lee was really Lee Maracle and that she just happened to be Ethel's neighbor. We met the next day at her house. The day after Lee Maracle and I just happened to be on the some plane to Penticton where Jeannette Armstrong and others met us at the airport and took us to the En'owkin Centre, which just happened on that day to be opening the International School of First Nations Writing (Sept. 11, 1989). I just happened to be their first guest speaker, relating to their apprehensive ears what I had to say about Native Writing in Canada. I was quite scared.

I began my presentation wishing the new students well and presenting to them a little wooden mountain climber, a moveable toy figure which climbs up if you pull the string that is looped through the hands and feet. I expressed my hope that the center would climb like this little fellow. For easy identification I attached one of the eagle feathers, then handed it over to Jeannette Armstrong. When I did that her eyes widened for a moment and I wondered what I had done wrong. Contrary to my fears I just happened to have done something right, I learned. Later Jeannette was scheduled to attend a ceremony the week after, and to that ceremony she needed to bring an eagle feather that had to be given to her. Time was getting close and she had no clue where the feather would come from – in this case it came from Germany. Since that first visit to the En'owkin Centre I have always felt very attached to the place and the people working there.

About a week later, while briefly visiting Fifth House publishers in Saskatoon together with my colleague from Kiel, Konrad Gross, two of the authors I hoped to interview just happened to phone within the span of about twenty minutes. Interviews were arranged with Maria Campbell in Saskatoon and Tomson Highway in Toronto. In Regina, I had a job interview at the Saskatchewan Indian Federated College, who just happened to be looking for someone to teach Canadian First Nations Literature. I got the job and a year later, with the support of the German Academic exchange Service, would go there with my family to teach at the SIFC for one wonderful and very rewarding year. Thank you, Bernie Selinger! A few days later in Winnipeg, I visited Pemmican Press, met Virginia Maracle and later that day, attended a meeting of writers and cultural workers who just happened that day to have the founding meeting of the Manitoba Native Writers Association. I also had the chance to interview Jordan Wheeler, the founder. At Thunder Bay I stayed with Renate Eigenbrod (who two years ago completed her PhD in Native Literature at the University of Greifswald) and she introduced me to authors Ruby (Farrell) Slipperjack and George Kenny, as well as to Ahmoo Allen Angeconeb, an Anishinabe artist who later became a very good friend and has visited us in Germany on several occasions. That fall trip through Canada culminated a very busy 24 hour stay in Toronto where I met with and interviewed Lenore Keeshig-Tobias, Beatrice Culleton (Mosionier) and Tomson Highway, and was also present at the book launch for Maria Campbell and Linda Griffith's *Book of Jessica*.

While conducting the interviews during that five week research trip in the fall of 1989, starting with the interview with Jeanette at the

En'owkin Centre, I had no clue they would eventually turn into a whole book, *Contemporary Challenges*, which included more conversations with Native authors conducted during my stay in Regina the following year. Nor did I know when visiting them, that Fifth House would agree to publish the book which came out in 1991 and was used in many university courses on Native Literature which began to be offered at that time (after Oka).

With that trip and the book project, I have again and again had the feeling that things "just happened" in extremely lucky and advantageous ways for me. Except for one individual poet, the Native authors I talked to were immensely supportive of the project. They simply told me go ahead. The 'moccasin telegraph' helped as well. Most of the writers I had conversations with, I have since seen on several occasions, both on Turtle Island and in Europe. Some have become personal friends. Do I hear someone say, "How subjective and unscholarly?" I wish I could see them more often. Since the lucky coincidences during my 1989 research trip just happened in wonderful, supportive and effective but inexplicable ways, I, as a "Westerner," had problems, to accept my good luck without continually asking for the why and how until one day Jeannette Armstrong, with an almost amused smile simply said, "Relax, Hartmut! That's just how things happen. It's all there. Just focus! Everything is there."

Thank you!

Water is Si^{w}lk^{w}

Composed for presentation at the World Water Forum in Kyoto, Japan, March 2003 on the opening plenary on behalf of UNESCO Canada

si^{w}lk^{w} she murmured   is an emergence   the subsequence of
all else   a completeness of the design   transforming to be lapped
continuously onto long pink tongues   in that same breathing   to
be the sweet drink coursing   to become the body   a welling spring
eternally renewing a sacred song   of the mother   vibrating outward
from the first minute drop formed of sky   earth   and light
bursting out of the deep   quietness si^{w}lk^{w} is a song she breathed
awakening cells   toward this knowing that you   are the Great River
as is   the abundant land   it brings   to carve its banks   then spread
its fertile plains and deltas and open its basins it's great estuaries
even to where it finally   joins   once again the grandmother ocean's
vast and liquid peace   as is the headwater glaciers of the jagged
mountains   waiting   for the yearly procession of thunder beings
bearing the dark cloud's sweep   upward   as spirits released from
green depths cradling whale song   dance on wind   as are the cold
ice springs feeding rushing brooks and willow draped creeks
meandering through teeming wetlands to sparkling blue lakes   as are
the silent   underground reservoirs coursing   gradually up
toward roots reaching down   to draw dew upward through countless
unfurlings   into the suns full light   as much as the salmon and
sleek sturgeon   sliding through strong currents   even the tall
straight reeds   cleaning stagnant pools   equally   are the marsh
bogs   swarming multitudinous glistening flagella and wings in high
country   holding dampness for the gradual descent through loam and
luxuriant life   to drink in   silk^{w} she said   is to remember   this
song is the way   it is the storms way   driving new wet earth
down slippery slopes   to make fresh land   the river's way heaving
its full silt weight   crushing solid rock   the tide's way
smoothing old plates of stone   finally deciding for all   the way of
ice   piled   bluegreen layer upon layer   over eons   sustaining
this fragment of now   so somewhere on her voluptuous body   the
rain continues   to fall   in the right places the mists unceasingly
float upward   to where they must   and the fog forever ghosts

across the land   in the cool desert wind   where no rain falls   and
each drop is more precious than   blood   balancing time   in the
way of the silvery hoar frost covering tundra   where iridescent ice
tinkles under the bellies of caribou   her song   is the sky's way
holding   the gossamer filaments of rainbow   together   guarding
the silent drift of perfect white flakes   where the moose stop momen-
tarily to look   upward   her song in the forest insuring a leaf shaped
just so   captures each glistening droplet   to celebrate   the vast
miles of liquid   pumping through the veins of the lion   parting
undulating savanna grasses   lifting great Condor wings   soaring
last circles in the mountains of Chile   accumulating in the places it
chooses   to pool in subterranean caverns   moving through porous
stones   seeping and wetting sand   deep   inside of her
caressing   thunder eggs and smooth pebbles at her heart
This song is the way

we come from a place of spirits

where all creation has spirit. each spirit connected by rhythms,
vibrations, songs, dances and stories
we carry in us memories of every creation story
we carry in us protocols
let's use these protocols
protocols that are based on respect
protocols that are based on peace
protocols that are based on love
let's really meet in a place of like minds
let's follow these protocols with like minds
with all creation
treating each other with respect
having peace
accepting love
talking to each other with respect
having peace
accepting love
walking to each other with respect
having peace
accepting love

we come from a place of spirits
not a place where we don't give a shit
about the next person
even if it's our mother
father
brother
sister
or cousin

we come from a place of spirits
where there is such a thing as karma
and "what goes around comes around"
we see this every day
like a slap in the face
the fire that blazed in the okanagan

all the trees who sacrificed their lives
let's call it a stand
let's call it resistance

resistance against mass destruction
mass homicide
mass genocide
resistance against corporations
corporations who sell the lives of many
by the truckload
that descend from mountains
one right after another
tree bodies slaughtered
stacked one on top of another
sawmills burned to the ground
trees burned to the ground
can we call this nature's resistance?
nature's struggle?
nature's protest?

we come from a place of spirits
let's take a moment of silence
for all the spirits that passed on

we come from a place of spirits
spirits that connect through heartbeat
through breath
through Creation
we are a pool of water
and if we dare to look in that pool
we will see
we will feel
we will know
that we are connected
what goes on here
goes on everywhere

we come from a place of spirits

a place we need to visit
a place we need to recognize
a place that exists in each of us
a place of beauty
a place of peace
a place of love
a place of respect
a place where you can go and never be turned away
a place where we can all dance
we can all celebrate
who we are

without illusions of
race
age
sex
demographics
money
because that's all it is
illusions
to divide us
to make us weak
to make war
to make governments
to conquer us
to make us dependant
on a system that clearly does not work
and has never worked
and no matter how we try to pass amendments
and no matter how we try to resist
and no matter how we try to protest
it just isn't enough
because of illusions
everyone is caught up in some sort of an illusion
that will always keep us divided
that will always keep us at war with one another
that will always keep us blind
and never see the truth

and never know the truth
and never feel the truth

we come from a place of spirits
and those spirits are calling us
and those spirits are dancing for us
and those spirits are singing for us
and those spirits are praying for us
to wake up
to wipe the illusions from our eyes
to come together with like minds
to come together with our protocols
our protocols of peace love and respect
these are basic laws

we come from a place of spirits
where everything is old
and everything is new
we learn from the old
we can reach back in time
learn from mistakes
our failure to communicate
our failure to use our protocols
we can really understand what the old people are saying
we can really understand what forgiveness means
we can really understand what cycles are
we can see that we are repeating cycles
dysfunctional cycles that we repeat, repeat and repeat
until we wake up

we come from a place of spirits
and I am here dancing singing and celebrating
who I am
who I am
who I am

Tribute to Natives That Died in 1918 (Flu Epidemic)

En'owkin class assignment 1996

Silent is the forest
Tales of days gone by
Marked graves in forgotten lands
Crosses rotted to the ground
Ancestors' cries
Lost in dull voices
Mothers buried beside their own
Newborn babes died with deadly force
Blood saturated the land
Boston's curse
Abyss of death
Enveloped the reserves
Grandfathers, who will hunt the land?
Roots lie decapitated
Medicine people, where are you?
Drums lie silent
Songs on the mournful winds.

Did you get my postcard from Mexico?

Dear friend, I've thought of you for the past three weeks. You always want to know where I am so I sent you a post card telling you why I didn't want to come home. I went to Mexico for solitude. I cried a lot while I was there thinking of the changes that were taking place in our Native communities. It seems the further I go away the more aware I become of who we are and why we hurt so much. When I was in Mexico, I saw people who had a lot of love for each other. Their language keeps them alive, material wealth did not matter, family is the main issue for these people. I thought about our people, how our families are divided and how we lost our love for each other. I just wanted to get lost into this scene. Although people talk to me in Spanish, I just smile and say no *Espanola englis*, I am a Navaho from Canada. I just wanted to escape the residential residue. I wanted to live with our people in the present but the past keeps holding them back. Joan, I am sure you got the post card that I sent from Hong Kong when I was teaching there. When I was dealing with sexual abuse issues, you were there. When I hit bottom, you were there. I walked away with a scar, held my face down, I was so crushed in spirit. Our people still suffer like that. Sometimes you need to go back in order to go ahead. I learned to love again. I was dead for along time, but today I help people that are hurting from their past. I can laugh, smile, touch, taste, hear myself laugh and sing. Joan, you won't get this postcard, but Brian will pick up your last mail, last words that were written to you. My friend you died July 23rd, 2003 and we buried you on the 29th. You didn't look like you, they had to put a mask on you. What kept me going was memories of your laughter, your words and how you treated your friends, your beautiful brown eyes. You attracted a lot of friends, you had a great heart. I was angry at how you died and what you fought against. You fought your last fight, you got your message across, you moved the people in the whole northern Saskatchewan, you were the Lady Diana of the North. They treated you with love and respect and also for the first time in history people came from all over to say good bye. Joan, I never say goodbye, forever we will remain friends. I have faith I will see you again, *Mahsi cho* for sharing your life with me, you gave me more reason to live and to love my people.

Suzi

Paddle My Canoe

Dark ghosts haunt house
Edge of the world
Walk along trail of unhappiness
Many have been down here

Felt those before us
Have prayed this day
Denied of authentic truth
Frames of empty words

A broken truth
Behind steel doors
White bright minds made a decision
In our best interest to follow this way

Uncomfortable in these skins
Deep entrenched hatred resentment
Decades go by silent even today
Caught in the middle of denial

No one takes control of their life
Some leave broken memories
Many want to roam endlessly
Send my spirit home land

something so simple
is the most difficult
a lot of people talk today
those who want to speak up

Mend the shattered mind
heal the scared heart
regenerate the physical
elevate the spirit

This – myself

Locked into myself where is the answer
Sucked into myself where is the freedom
Fearful of myself when do I let go
Fighting myself when do I set myself free
Letting myself go I have so much to learn

I'm letting myself be free for the first time
I'm not giving up on myself ever again
I'm moving forward
I'm unraveling the mystery inside
I'm going to begin to understand myself
I'm going to find the courage to go through with this!
I'm not stopping until I find out who I am
This – myself I love
This – myself I comprehend
This – myself I am proud
This – myself I have dignity
This – myself I have self-respect
This – myself I have confidence
This – myself I can do anything I dream
This – myself I have found who I am
This – myself no one can take anything from me
I know who I am

Four Invisible Circles

It is safer with you far from me
Not bare witness to such horror
Your eyes are to behold beauty
Not a heathen child with scars

I have everything to offer
None can I offer you

I am alone once more
Fending for noone's affection

I wander this empty trail
With no hand to hold

Keep me in harmony
In balance
Stand by me
Don't let me drown

Natural forces will have their way
Earth and universe discuss
How they look upon us
What lays beneath the surface

Accept the love I have for you in my soul
That alone is not enough
Even for ten lifetimes
I love You with all my heart

These words alone will not bear fruit
I have no way to stand
Only the stars and spirits to guide us

You are there
Out of reach

I am here
Empty to the touch

The universe has been kind
So very generous to both of us

We are torn from a lovers cloth
How we differ
How we are the same

Lake has dried
No music
Still waters
Empty silent air

What is Writing but the Wild Horses of Your Thoughts?

Thundering from your mind with the power of hooves and snorting,
frothing at the mouth as I sit typing
as fast as I can just to keep up

Taste the dust in your mouth and look over your shoulder
I can see them!
They are coming for me!
Like clouds dropping from the New Mexico sky
A tornado hangs on the horizon

Certain whispers will keep you awake at night
So write it out goddammit!
Smell the hay in the air
They are still here, breathing steam

It is our own afterworld we are after
Where quiet time arrives like a wave from the lake
settling into the sand, kissing the shore
with a wet tongue
The sand cradles my feet
and the wind tosses my hair around my head
like a wild pony shaking her mane

I am alive with the smell of horses
I can feel their breath
Hot and moist
breathing on the nape of my neck
Breathing and whispering
crazy stories in my ears
What is writing but the wild horses of your thoughts?

The Ninety Dollar Surrender

Precis: This is the fictionalized story of Mary Eleanor Williams, the oldest daughter of a St. Peter's Indian Band Councillor. She is fourteen and frightened at the prospect of leaving her reserve. However, there is no choice for her family or the community; they must leave. The wagon journey to their new home is fraught with emotional upheaval and physical danger. Mary must contend with the rigors of the trip, an awakening womanhood and the sorrow of a forced move

Chapter 1

March 12, 1908

The sky is getting darker and there are more gusts of wind. A late storm is coming. I turn to go inside when a harsh swirl of wind strikes the dead oak tree out back and throws it against the fence. I get my little sister Abigail and baby brother Colin into the house just as the first hailstones begin to fall. Thunk. Thunk. Thunk. From the window, I can see a ridge of dark grey clouds moving in from the southwest.

Mother has an armful of blankets. "Mary. Get the hammer and nails," she yells over the pounding on the roof. I stumble to the kitchen and search the cupboard where Father keeps the tools. My hands shake when I hand over the hammer.

I am fourteen. My family lives on the St. Peter's Indian Band Reserve located next to the town of Selkirk in southern Manitoba. Earlier that day, I watched my father and Uncle Gordie ride off in the wagon to a neighbour's place. Changes began when the Indian Affairs men came last fall. There were three of them. Two with fat, sweaty faces. "Too greedy," whispered Mother the day we saw them. The other man was stick-thin and dressed in grey flannel; he did all the talking. They stayed in Selkirk for nearly four months. At the end of December, our band held a vote and, the thin man announced that the St. Peter's Band had voted to move to a new reserve. Everyone was worried now. That was not what they had voted on and this was the third meeting this week.

Mother held out her hand for a nail. I pull out a straight one and give it to her. Our rhythm is set like that until every window is blanketed. The little kids are good. They sit huddled on our old green couch, nodding solemnly each time I hiss, “Stay where you are.” When we are finished, the house is too dark so Mother lights a kerosene lamp. Warm yellow light chases away the dimness and I feel a little better.

I know Mother is worried about our father and her brother Gordie out there in the awful hailstorm. She paces the living room with her arms held tightly in front. Her shadow marches across the dim walls behind her. I wish she would stop the constant walking. Colin and Abigail begin to cry softly. I want to cry too.

“Do you think it'll last long?” I whisper.

My mother’s brown woolen skirt swishes against floor. The quiet sobs of my siblings and the rattle on the roof are the only other sounds. She had not heard me. I spoke louder.

“Mother. Do you think the storm is going to be over soon?”

She turns toward me. There is a sparkle of tears at the inner corners of her eyes that tells me she is trying hard not to cry. Then I realize what she is thinking. Hail like this can kill a person.

Last year, a sudden storm like this one caught poor little Mitchell Sanderson out on the open road between his place and town. He’d been sent to town for sugar. They found him a few yards from a big oak tree with his body protecting a sack of sugar for the cakes his mother wanted to bake. Poor Mrs. Sanderson still blamed herself for that.

As though only realizing we are there, my mother rushes over and takes Colin from me. Abigail moves closer too.

“Of course. Yes. It’ll be over soon, Mary.”

She holds Colin as if he is a newborn baby, murmuring sounds that calm us all. My little brother soon falls asleep. Abigail sits quietly, watching her every movement.

Finally, the storm is over. The clatter on the roof dwindles to a few patters and an eerie silence soon falls over the house. My mother and I let out great breaths of air. We smile at each other. I giggle and that sets us both to laughing aloud. The sound of our laughter is strange to hear. Colin wakes up with a sleepy smile. Abigail’s delicate giggles are added to the ruckus, when into our happiness comes a loud knock on the door.

“Daddy home,” squealed Colin as he tries to wriggle out of Mother’s arms.

I knew it wasn't Father. Why would he knock? My mother knew too. She put Colin down on the floor and turned him toward us. Thankfully, Abigail took her brother. She carried him over to an old wood trunk by the wall and put an old blanket over both of them like a tent. I could hear her whisper, "Let's go to fish camp," (a game I had played with her). With my heart pounding I moved to stand in front of the makeshift tent. Mother opens the door and sunlight sends a long sliver of light inside.

Two strangers stood on our steps. White men. One had bushy eyebrows and a grey beard, the other was red-faced and wheezing. Greybeard asked, "Is Mr. Williams was home?"

Mother shook her head no and explained that he had gone to see a neighbour. After a brief discussion, Redface held out a thick brown envelope. I saw my mother's arm falter as she reached across the doorway into the bright sunshine. Both men nod curtly then turn to leave. I ran to the door to get a better look at them. Town was six miles away. I wondered how they weren't caught in the hailstorm.

Out in the yard their horses stomped, crushing the balls of ice around them. White gusts of breath shoot from their nostrils. They are skittish but not because of any storm. Our dog Patch is bothering them. She darts in for a nip then runs out of the way when the horses kick out. One of the men (it looks to be Redface) stamps his foot and yells a curse. Patch doesn't seem to care and keeps at the horse's legs until they are well past the fence. The storm must have missed the men by mere minutes.

"Patch," I call. "Come on back girl."

After a few more attacks against the horses that are answered by the shouts of the men, Patch races back into the yard. I knelt down as she came up to me, her pink tongue lolls to one side dripping saliva onto me. A stub of tail that was bitten off in a skirmish with a black bear moves in a black whir. I hold her close and bury my face in the rough fur not understanding why I feel so proud of the dumb mutt.

I don't know how long I stayed like that. The clink of a harness and hooves ringing out meant my Father and Uncle Gordie were coming back. Soon they come into the yard with the team at a near gallop. Steam clouds around the massive brown bodies of our two old horses when they pull to a stop. My father leaps down and runs toward the house. The look in his eyes scares me, there is fear in there again.

I can't get used to seeing that in his eyes.

Patch wriggles out of my grasp to meet him but Father barely glances at her. I stood to wait for him. As he comes near, my heart beats faster.

"Anything happen here?" he asks gruffly.

I nod, mute and suddenly very afraid of the harmless looking envelope which my mother had taken. The hand my father puts on my shoulder trembles. The cold inside me gets colder. I put my own small hand on top of his big one then hold on tightly. Uncle Gordie calls out that he'll take care of the horses. As one, my father and I go inside.

Inspiration for The Ninety Dollar Surrender:

In 1907, the Manitoba Government and the settlers of Selkirk conspired to steal the rich farmlands of the St. Peter's Band through a shady land development deal. In what has now been found to be an illegal surrender, the Saulteaux and people lost their homes, farms and most of their possessions in the forced move to the bush lands of the Interlake region. Ninety dollars is the amount which Frank Pedley, Deputy Superintendent General of Indian Affairs at the time, said would be paid to the head of every family for each acre of land. A land developer in charge of the transactions disappeared with all the money and many people were left with nothing. Indian Affairs commissioners in Ottawa turned a blind eye to the unlawful actions of their officials. St. Peter's band members moved to their new reserve by train, wagon, on horseback and by foot. Several people died on the journey. Today, the town of Selkirk sits on what was once the St. Peter's Reserve, the home of Chief Peguis who was named The Great Peacemaker by the Canadian public for his intervention in a planned slaughter of early Selkirk settlers during the mid-1800's.

Dry Lips Oughta Move to America

It's no secret that the three largest human exports to the United States are hockey players, comedians and Native playwrights (or by proxy their Native plays). Practically unknown in the States, most researchers and the few hardy theater eccentrics often had to look northward to get their Aboriginal theater fix.

That is why I found myself on a cold New England evening, making my way through the narrow streets of Providence, Rhode Island to see a public reading of my play, *THE BUZ'GEM BLUES*, an Aboriginal comedy. On January 24th, Trinity Repertory Theater, one of the five largest repertory theaters in America with an annual budget of 7.6 million dollars, hosted its second annual 'Theater From The Four Directions Festival'. Last year's festival, now an anticipated yearly event, included Assiniboine/Nakota playwright William Yellow Robe Jr. (who is now the company's Playwright-in-Residence), and two Canadian Native writers, Saulteaux playwright and winner of the 1997 Governor General's Award, Ian Ross (who for some reason neglected to show up), and myself.

Representatives from theaters and educational institutions in America's northeast came to the sold out Festival to check out this strange animal called Native theater. Based on the success of both festivals, plans for a full scale production of one of these plays is anticipated for next season with a possible national tour to follow. It will be the largest production of a Native play seen in America. As Cherokee director and Yale School of Drama, graduate Elizabeth Theobald Richards puts it, "it will definitely be one for the record books."

While relatively rare, Aboriginal involvement in theater is not entirely unknown in America. Within its own borders, Native American Indian writers like Diane Glancy, William Yellow Robe Jr. and Hanay Geiogama have been plying their artistic wares for years with limited results in an environment that was unaware there were still Native people alive in America, let alone that they had anything interesting to say on stage.

Randy Reinholz, Artistic Director and co-founder with Jean Bruce Scott of Native Voices, an American Indian theater company and Festival located in San Diego and Los Angeles, believes he knows why. "I'd say Native Theater in the States is like Native people in the

States. We're struggling to have anybody notice we are not extinct. While we were doing (Canadian playwright) Maria Clement's show 'URBAN TATTOO' at the Gene Autry Heritage Museum in L.A., the museum did a market survey of what the common perceptions about Native Americans in Los Angeles and Southern California were. The most common perception is that they didn't know there were Native people; they thought they were extinct. So when you think that is what popular Americans think, the idea of Native theater is really way out there. It is a kind of esoteric thing."

Oskar Eustis, Artistic director of Rhode Island's Trinity Repertory Theater, has a similar spin on the theory. "...in the United States, there is a much lower level of sophistication about culture, about the idea that the government should be involved with it in an ongoing investment and supportive of. So any group that doesn't have financial resources or critical masses, it makes it tougher for them to find a voice in entering the mainstream. As a result, I feel like we haven't gotten a movement here yet.... I look at Tomson Highway's breakthrough plays in the mid eighties events that seemed to catalyze Canadian Native theater. We haven't had that founding bomb go off."

But the bomb may be ticking. These days, the Native theatrical voice seems to be appearing disproportionately more often south of the border; but, it is a Canadian Native voice. Reinholz's Native Voices, in operation since 1993, has workshopped and presented twenty-four scripts in total. About half were by Canadian Native playwrights. The company is in preproduction for their third Equity production in L.A. and two of those three productions features Canadian writers.

Oddly enough, the presence of Canadian Native writers in the American theater system is not going unnoticed. Reinholz's Board of Directors have been known to complain about the high percentage of Canadians this American organization seem to be supporting. During the late nineties, I was invited twice to participate in the Prince William Sound Community College Edward Albee Theater Conference held in Valdez, Alaska. The reason I was there was to accept (both times) first prize in the Alaska Native Plays Contest. During my last visit, one of the organizers told me the rules for the competition were going to change. A higher up at the University of Alaska faculty who organized the conference asked with some irritation, "Are we just going to become a dumping ground for Canadian Indian playwrights?"

"Canadian Native writers have a greater history, a longer history of combining storytelling with contemporary theater. The scripts are easier to work with because the writers have a long history of working in theater. When we work with a lot of the writers from the States, I would say with half of them it is their first or second workshop. So there was a kind of getting everybody on the same page process of 'what do you do to workshop'. The Canadians had already been through this process, very familiar with the process and very able to use it properly," comments Reinholz. "The writers have been known for a while. Canadian writers have been published and people have been writing about Canadian Native theater for ten years. It's part of the mainstream. There's also a deeper talent pool. I think there's an emerging directing, and I bet there'll be a designing pool and stage managers. So there's quite an interesting pool to draw from in Canada," adds Reinholz.

The end result of this Canadian First Nation theatrical influx into the American theatrical heart... Who knows? It might end up being just a momentary blip on the scope, or, it might actually develop into a legitimate trend. It is too early to say. Time will tell and more research is necessary.

In a further search for Native theater in America, after Rhode Island I saddled up my pony and forayed to the next logical destination in my theatrical sojourn – New York City's Broadway. Rarely will you find more theaters and plays per capita than in the theater district around Times Square. As was expected, there was nary a Native play to be seen anywhere. Perhaps that's why it's called the Great White Way.

However, that part of the journey was not without discovery. New York's Smithsonian Museum of the American Indian is planning to further explore the possibility of incorporating and utilizing more Native theater into their mandate. On an ironic note, the museum is located at the edge of Wall Street, which got it's name several hundred years ago because there was originally a large wall built on that location to keep out the Indians. On an even more ironic note, while at the Smithsonian Museum of the American Indian I bumped into, of all people, the Honorable Robert Nault, the Canadian Federal Minister of Indian and Northern Development.

I guess the Department of Indian Affairs has to know what all the Indians are up to, regardless of where they are.

Recreational Cultural Appropriation

F. Scott Fitzgerald once wrote, "The Rich are different from you and I," to which people usually respond, "Yeah, they got more money." On a similar theme, it's been my Ojibway- tainted observation over the years that "Middle Class White people are different from you and I"... yeah, they're insane.

Much has been written over the years about the differences between Native people and non-Native people, and how differently they view life. I think there's no better example of this admittedly broad opinion than in the peculiar world of outdoor recreational water sports and the death wish that surrounds it. As a member of Canada's Indigenous population, I've always cast a suspicious glance at all these water-logged enthusiasts for several reasons. The principal one being the now familiar concept of cultural appropriation - this time our methods of water transportation. On any given weekend, Canadian rivers are jam packed with plastic/fiberglass kayaks and canoes, practically none of them filled with authentic Inuit or Native people, all looking to taunt death using an Aboriginal calling card.

Historically, kayaks and canoes were the lifeblood of most Native and Inuit communities. They were vital means of transportation and survival, not toys to amuse beige, bored weekend warriors. To add insult to injury and further illustrate my point, there's a brand of gloves used by kayakers to protect their hands from developing callouses. There are called Nootkas. To the best of my knowledge, the real Nootka, a West Coast First Nation, neither kayaked nor wore gloves.

Perhaps my argument can best be articulated with an example of the different way these two cultural groups react to a single visual stimulus. First, in a river put some Native people in a canoe right beside some White people, also in a canoe. Directly in front of them should be a long stretch of roaring rapids. With large pointy rocks and lots and lots of turbulent white water. Now watch the different reactions.

Granted, I'm being a bit general but I can safely say that the vast majority of Native people, based on thousands of years of traveling the rivers of this great country of ours, would probably go home and order a pizza. Or, put the canoe in their Ford pickup and go downstream to a more suitable and safe location, and pick up pizza on the way.

Usually, the only whitewater Native people prefer is in their showers. Hurtling toward potential death and certain injury tends to go against many traditional Native beliefs. Contrary to popular belief, the word portage is not a French word, it is Native for "Are you crazy?! I'm not going through that! Do you know how much I paid for this canoe?"

Now put some sunburned Caucasian canoeists in the same position and their natural inclination is to aim directly for the rapids paddling as FAST as they can TOWARD the white water. I heard a rumor once that Columbus was aiming his three ships directly at a raging hurricane when he discovered the Bahamas. I believe I have made my point. Yet even with this bizarre lemming-like behavior, there are still more White people out there than Native people.

I make these observations based on personal experience. Recently, for purely anthropological reasons, I have risked my life to explore this unique sub-culture known as whitewater canoeing and sea kayaking. There is also a sport known as whitewater kayaking but I have yet to put that particular bullet in my gun. So for three days I found myself in the middle of Georgian Bay during a storm, testing my abilities at sea kayaking. I, along with a former Olympic rower, a Québécois lawyer who consulted on the Russian Constitution, one of Canada's leading Diabetes specialists and a 6 ft. 7 ex-Mormon who could perform exorcisms bonded over four foot swells and lightening. All in all, I think a pretty normal cross-cut of average Canadians. The higher the waves, the more exciting they found it.

I often find these outings to be oddly patriotic in their own unique way. I cannot tell you the number of times I've seen many of these people wringing out their drenched shirts, showing of an unusual array of tan lines, usually a combination of sunburnt red skin, and fish- belly white stomachs. For some reason, it always reminds me of the red and white motif on the Canadian flag. Maybe, back in the 1960's, that is where the Federal government got their original inspiration for our national emblem.

But this is only one of several sports originated by various Indigenous populations that have been corrupted and marketed as something fun to do when not sitting at a desk in some high rise office building. The Scandinavian Sami, also known as Lapplanders, were very instrumental in the development of skiing, although I doubt climbing to the top of a mountain and hurling themselves off to make it to the bottom as fast as gravity and snow would allow was not a cultural activity. The same could be said for bungee jumping. Originally, it was a coming of age ritual in the south Pacific. Young boys would build platforms, tie a vine to their leg and leap off to show their bravery and passage into adulthood. I doubt the same motivation still pervades the sport (if it can be called a sport).

I have brought up this issue of recreational cultural appropriation many times with a friend who organizes these outdoor adventures. The irony is that she works at a hospital. And she chews me out for not wearing a helmet while biking. She says there is no appropriation. If anything the enthusiasm for these sports is a sign of respect and gratefulness.

I think these people should pay a royalty of sorts every time they try to kill themselves using one of our cultural legacies. I'm not sure if a patent or copyright was ever issued on kayaks or canoes (it was probably conveniently left out of some treaty somewhere) but somebody should definitely investigate that possibility. Or better yet, every time some non-Native person whitewater canoes down the Madawaska River or goes kayaking off of Tobermory they first should take an Aboriginal person to lunch. That is a better way to show respect and gratefulness (and it's less paperwork).

Everybody's Lookin' for Sammy

Dedicated to Sammy Douglas of the STO:LO Nation

everybody everybody everybody's lookin' for lookin' for sammy
down by the river
down by the river side
cause he was doing what he loved to do best
and he was doing what he fought to do
now everybody everybody's lookin' for lookin' for sammy
down by the river,
down by the riverside,
yaayaayaayaayaayaayaahaahaahaahaahaa
cause he was doing what he loved to do best
yaayaayaayaayaayaaaaaaahaahaa
he was doing what he fought to do
yayayayayayaya
he was fishing
he was fishing fishing fishing
fishing for salmon down by the riverside
down by the river
down by the river
down by the riverside
yayaayaaayaahaahaahaahaahaahaa

Too Wicked

A straight pow-wow song plays on the stereo and I give him a big smile. "Charlie please don't, I'm not comfortable with that," I say in a little girl voice that I hate. I'm in love. I love everything about him. I want to let him go down on me because I have fantasized about it so much. Instead I say, "You don't have to do that," and pull him on top of me.

"Just love me Charlie."

He says, "Helen, I love everything about you."

I will love my cowboy forever but, I don't believe him or myself. I don't spread my legs for aliens and anal probes, only for handsome Indian men. I can make them happy.

Charlie drops me off at home. I kiss him and he gives me a hug that makes me feel safe and strong. Nothing is wrong with the world. Nothing is wrong with me. I get out of the truck and avoid looking into his sweet gentle eyes.

"Take care, Charlie."

I wish that he will come back and marry me. I think about what I've said to him, replaying my words over and over in my mind.

I moved back to the reserve after my parents passed away into my granny's old house. I belong here. The people accepted me back even though I'm a Bill C 31, a reinstated Indian, a half-breed. I go out to the porch and look out on the reserve. My relatives love me and I love them. They give me the space I need. My cousins say I have the cleanest house. I think my obsessive cleanliness is a result of my mother's residential school experience. I still hear Mom. "Don't eat like a savage. Don't be a dirty Indian." Those Grey nuns brainwashed and shamed her. My dad was the worst when in a drunken rage he would scream, "Stupid squaws. Whores. Cunts."

Mom could be a hoot, she had a great sense of humor. Dad thought he was marrying an obedient Indian woman. I don't know what happened to him as a child but I'm sure that the war warped his brain. I can't remember him ever laughing. Mom thought she was eloping with a savior and getting a better life beyond a reserve where she had to ask permission from the Indian agent to leave.

Someone once told my mom that her dad walked on the prairies for two days after she eloped. He didn't want her to marry a white man. He saw her intelligence and wanted more for her. He could see my father's war demons. My father did have integrity and died telling us he loved us. He asked us for forgiveness. I gave it to him. How could I be angry? He was human. My mother, even though a chronic alcoholic, gave me the greatest gift: she taught me to pray.

My parents loved me. I love them. It all is so complicated. I never know how to feel. Sometimes I talk to the drug and alcohol counselor about my problems but, I find forgetting much easier.

I walk outside to the porch and sit in a lawn chair. I ache for Charlie and my loneliness sweeps out to the stars. I call on my grandmother to lift me up to the Holy place where the Creator, Star people, and all my relations pray, sing, dance and weep for their crazy children below. I want to feel clean. I need help to become a real person, not a phony or a slut. I'm a impostor and only the Creator knows how bad I am. I am to be denied true love. I love Charlie but I have to let him go before I kill his soul like they did to me. I want to cry. I feel it in my throat. I have to push it away. I will only hurt him when he rejects me. I can't allow myself that. For his safety I can't let him in. I will never be with him again. I'm so grateful for the one night. He is a good man from a good family. I know it's just not right. I yearn for him already.

I love to write but I burn it before anyone can read it. Only the spirits read my work.

I am the accountant for the band. I love to sit at my desk and figure out the riddle of numbers. Today is Friday and I'm going to the city tonight to get away from the reserve.

It only takes a few hours to get there. I get off the bus and walk downtown to skid row. My brown sisters need my help. I blend in easily – Indian woman, braids, tee shirt, granny sweater, jeans, sneakers, and carrying a plastic bag. At the seedy Sundance Hotel a balding man with tar-stained teeth and brown fingers sits behind a desk. I see it in his eyes. He is a fucking pervert. All he sees is brown skin and a pussy.

"I need a room. How much?"

"For you sweetheart, fifty bucks or free if you give me head."

I smile sweetly, hand him fifty dollars and see my hands tear into his guts.

"I work weekends if you change your mind. Got ID? Where you from honey?"

I hand him my late cousin's identification. She's been dead four years. Murdered. We look alike. He writes down her name and status number then hands me a key. Room 120.

"My home is the earth and the sky," I say.

He shoots me a look that shows an apparent lack of respect for me. *Is it because of the color of my skin?* He presses a button that buzzes like a wasp and a door going to the rooms unlocks.

"Fucking smarty ass squaw," he mumbles.

I open the door and go upstairs. Shit. The room sits right on top of the bar. Country music vibrates through a red cigarette burned carpet. The room is clean enough, a single bed and no television or phone. At least it has a sink and a toilet. I open my bag and take out a change of clothes, toothbrush and my hunting knife. Stupid fucks named the bar after something sacred. No wonder they get the creeps, the chronic and the hopeless.

I wash my face, then grab the knife. It is small but sharp. I put it in my back pocket with my sweater covering it and go downstairs to the pub. It smells of pinesol and piss in there. I order a beer and scan the room. *The Creator will lead me to the right man.* I see my Aunt Delia sitting in the corner, drunk and oblivious. Auntie hasn't been the same since her son hung himself in a closet. He was only thirty four.

At Jason's wake, I sat next to my aunty Delia and the rest of his relatives. Between the great wailing and tears we laughed over the happy times. Uncle Grant talked about the horse and buggy days when he needed a pass from the Indian Agent to leave the reserve; when liquor laws were strict; and when snakes sang to my Holy grandmother. Jason had many friends, was a bookworm, was great with horses, and was funny as hell. But he drank too much and became his own worst enemy. Cousin Kathy was in town a few days before he died. She said she saw Jason in the back of a police cruiser. He caught her eye and waved like the Queen Mother. She said he had the wave down pat. She couldn't stop laughing. That was Jason. My favorite cuz. My sunshine, and my moon.

Jason was raging drunk, throwing rocks as I ran from his drunken curses. I ran to the river and dove in. I was a lone beaver swimming in still water. I see the slash scars on his face. He is hanging in a closet of atoms, genetics jumbled, Indian ancestor's memory gone. In my profound mourning I hack off my finger in one blow. It is painless, a small sacrifice. At the wake he stared at me through an open window and whispered a story about the night *they* circled him then pissed on him. "Dirty drunken Indian living off taxpayers money." After the funeral I remain at Jason's grave, crying and pouring beer onto his thirsty grave.

I remember how I tried to bring Auntie home on my last trip to the city but she ditched me. Sitting next to her is one of the wicked men. I know he is one of them and I need to save her. I stare at him with a look that says "come fuck me, baby." His eyes move from my face to my breasts to my legs. He walks over like he is real good but he reeks of cheap cologne, has false teeth and wears a wide open shirt that displays a revolting hairy, acne ridden chest. I notice that his moustache is like Custers.

"Honey can I buy you a drink?" he asks.

In his mouth I see maggots. *Sure, you hairy fuck.*

"I would love a drink."

I can't stand it when old dirty men hit on me. I tried to explain it to Charlie once but he didn't understand how it is to be an Indian woman.

"Indian women are prey to the perverts of the world," I proclaimed. "I'm a respectable woman. I work in the band office. I'm smart. I dress modestly, and I'm only thirty. But I can't walk down the city street. Cars will stop and drivers ask "how much?" They look at me in the same way. I'm inhuman, a piece of dirt. They look through me like I'm nothing, just a squaw."

Charlie just smiled at me. "It's just because you're beautiful and stink pretty." He never seems to take issues seriously.

I kiss my Auntie goodbye but she is drunk and doesn't recognize me. She tells me to piss off.

He says his name is John. I lead him out the back door into the alley. When I look at the sky through the city lights I can see stars and the Northern lights dancing for me. We stand behind an open trash bin. He unbuttons my pants and kneels in front of me as if I were his God. I let him go down on me.

He looks at me the same way my father did.

"That was good baby."

He stands up, takes a ten doller bill out of his pocket and waves it in front of my face. "You're going to have to work for this whore," he hisses like a badger.

I kneel down and unzip his pants. I want to puke. He grabs my hair and pushes himself into my mouth. I grab my knife and in shame beg I Creator for forgiveness.

"Great One forgive me," I scream like a two year old while I hack at him.

A little person in buckskin watches me and cries out, "But they just want love."

John falls backwards in shock. Blood spurts from him and he begs for mercy from his Indian squaw. He hears the wailing of spirits who surround us with Great Mystery. A police car comes down the alley. Spirits unseen cover their eyes, and his blood becomes water on my clothes.

I go back into the Sundance and take Auntie out of the bar. The clerk presses his magic button to open the door so we can go up to my room.

He mumbles, "Fucking Indian lesbos. I knew you were a dyke."

I lay Auntie down on the bed and fall asleep on the floor. When I wake up on Sunday afternoon, Auntie is gone. Was she here? Sometimes when I think I am awake I'm only dreaming. The old man told me I could walk in many worlds like the Sasquatch does.

I get off the midnight bus and walk the few miles to the reserve. In the darkness, I look up at the stars and imagine that the stars are singing around a drum. I feel in my heart the integrity of our people and of the world. Holy peace is redeemed, born from an eagle whistle. I am like a warrior. I will return to the battlefield that rages in the cities.

As a child I was afraid of everything. No longer. The Creator loves his children. I thank my lovers who have never heard my prayers nor held my hand during a ceremony. A regal sparkle of light once danced kindly over my head and taught me how to chase lost demons into a bad medicine box. I don't have any luck with men. The old man promised me to the Holy one. I see him in my dreams.

This is my Holy song to the One Creator.
Great One committed to you oh my Creator
my Children believe in you through the darkness
alone in the darkness I pray that is all that matters
awake and my hangover sweeps out to the stars

and cosmos calling by name Holy grandmothers
and grandfathers to lift me to the love of
the mystery Creator Man From Above
help me in my numbness I'm afraid of you
The pregnant rattlesnake begged my grandmother
not to kill her, "Like you people there are good and
bad snakes. Don't kill me for the sins of others."

Blues

My girl
It's all gone
remember where we used to pick
nothing left
stumps clear-cut
I was surprised
at all the bush gone
I kept going along the road
then just about to Little Sandy
I found where they stopped cutting
I was able to pick a few blue berries
it scares me
pretty soon
there is going to be no place left
for us to pick.

Mathilda Frazer - August 22, 2003

Ohpahowipisim – Flying Up Moon
August 16, 1977

Gently, the picker
charms life off branches
cradles the small gift to her breast
grateful for life
the picker lifts her berries to the winds
then lays her offering in a place untouched.

The first berry to offer itself after a long winter
is the heart berry
the strawberry awakens the sleeper.

Raspberry
must be coaxed to drop its fruit
by thunder and lightening.

Blueberries like hot days
        Ohpahowipisim – Flying Up Moon
        to ripen
        that velvety blue divide.

Tart cranberries ripen
when the leaves dissolve
        into golden hues with crimson highlights
        and fingers will numb to beat the snowflakes
        to gather the last offerings of summer.

A picker
never stays too long in one place
gathering here and there
always in search of a patch full with berries.

A seasoned picker
lifts her pail to the sky
lets the wind
        do the cleaning
carries away twigs and leaves
and adds the berries together.

Not one berry will pass my lips
        before the frost touches them
after we have gathered
I will feast on the last handful
and savor each sweet juicy
azure kiss of creation.

There is calm silence in the bush
where thoughts
meander around trees
rattling leaves
while bees buzz around
adding their two bits.

In a thicket of purple blue haze
where soft velvet incandescent
the reflection of blueberries
smothers the afternoon into its folds
reminds me of how beautiful I am
infused amongst the birch
and spruce laden with bear claw cones.

There they are
Blueberry queens
mom and grandma
bumps high in the air
in slow motion their hips sway
lost in a wonderful blue world
of togetherness.

At night
when you close your eyes
you can still see them
little blue spirits
I see radiant blue florescent dancing lights
some see giant grapes
others floating blueness.

I adjust the dial on the car radio
Transforming airwaves into sound
a man's voice
says "Elvis is dead!"
found at Graceland in his pj's
'Blue Suede Shoes' fills the silence
a stone sinks
        further into my being
        deeper than I ever felt
        bluer than I ever been.

I yell my news
to Mom who stops to tell grandma
who Elvis was

grandma said she knew him as the man
who looked like a handsome Cree.

When people ask me
where were you when Elvis died?
I will say
busy tickling blueberries
off their branches
without touching them

My girl
It's all gone
remember where we used to pick
nothing left
stumps clear-cut
I was surprised
at all the bush gone
I kept going along the road
then just about to Little Sandy
I found where they stopped cutting
I was able to pick a few blue berries
it scares me
soon
there is going to be no place left
for us to pick

Mathilda Frazer - August 22, 2003

Hell No

Bounced around the issues
bore no opinion
no one ever asked what I thought.

Came from a long line of
        don't say anything
        just leave it alone.

Smiled like the Mona Lisa
as I was sliced and diced.

Because I could
        I did just that
and into the sunset I arrived.

Found voices
        that resonated
        danced
        that were confident
        gifted
        some voices were loud yet empty.

I found my voice
buried in the muskeg
it was there all this time
        all the while I searched in the silence
        and in the darkness
        my voice
is where I had left it
after setting rabbit snares.
It was a strong voice
loud and clear
        even carried a tune.

I knew I could and I did
began to speak for the plants
        ensure roots were intact
they even began to grow out of my back
I tried to hide them
but the branches grew thicker
deeper into the dirt
my roots took hold amongst
                the old rocks.

I outgrew my safe space

Saw children
        beg for food
        while slot machines
                stole grandparents
ate up communities
and spit out jealousy and greed

No matter how I much
        I pounded my fist
        pointed fingers
shook my head to say – Hell No!

The earth eating monsters
        shifting gears
        ate everything in sight
        drank up all the water
        devoured whole stands of trees in three minutes
        destroyed my pharmacy, my food supply for generations

winds grew violent
fish bubbled to the surface
white moose charged
white raven shrieked
white cougar hissed
and white buffalo kicked up dirt

heartbeats still sound
words were power
graceful bodies under pressure emerged
and our dreams came true.

Window (Lyrics from CD "Red")

I wish I had a window
So I could see
The moon rise
Full body above me
And she'll move my waters
Like the sea
I wish I wish I
Had a window

But I will be dreaming of home
I will be traveling
In sleep
Unraveling
Each moment each hour
While the milkweed is grown
To flower
I will be traveling

I wish I had a door
That I could use
I'll leave it open a crack
For the spring to
Flow through
And swing it open wide
When the summer is new
Well I wish I wish I
Had a door

But I will be coming home soon
I will be traveling
In sleep
Between moments
Unraveling
Each hour each day
While blooms
Seeds to decay
I will be traveling

Section 5

Dramatic Writings

Four monologues from *"A Windigo Tale"*

"A Windigo Tale," the story of an Aboriginal woman, Doris, who is given a second chance to defend her daughter, Lily, against the evil Windigo spirit that consumed their lives. Pressed by her old auntie, Evelyn, Doris elicits the help of Lily's boyfriend, David, to exorcise the spirit of her abusive Windigo-Husband.

DORIS

(Spot up on Doris as Glen Miller's "String of Pearls" comes up.) Do you remember when you came to see me and took me out on the town, and we danced and danced. The band played that song I liked so much. **(Hums "String of Pearls," Dances.)** I was wearin' my new dress. First new dress I ever owned. I first saw it walkin' past Simpson Sears, and I thought oh, I'd love that dress. I closed my eyes, held my breath, and could actually see myself in it, dancin' with you. And so I decided, I would have it! I had to, because it meant more to me than just a dress, it meant a new life, a new beginnin'. It was what they called a midnight blue, and had these little chiffon petals woven into the material. You complimented me and put your hands around my waist. So small, you said, like a child's. **(She stands and moves as though looking at herself in a full length mirror)** And that's when you proposed. You were working steady and making good money. Me, I'd been used to hard times. You were my way out. Or were you? – I'd wanted to become part of the big crowd strolling up and down Yonge Street, the longest street in the world! But you were gonna bring me back here! Oh no, I didn't want that, but, all the same, I said, Okay, I'll marry you. But you have to promise me one thing: to be a good man. My poor father, bless him, never hurt a fly, he respected life. That's what I said I wanted more than anything, a good man. And you said, I am, and then I said, I do. **(Exit Doris, who shuffles off stage. Music goes down as CBC Radio announcer comes up. Light up.)**

DAVID

(Spot up, David begins to read from his book. The sound of wind may be used.) The Windigo belief resides in actual experience which is said to take many forms. While cannibal ideas, thoughts, anxieties and stories were a traditional and accepted part of the belief system of Native culture, nevertheless, the cannibal act was perceived with fear and horror. An important element in the Windigo belief is spirit possession. The individual regarded as a case of Windigo Psychosis is one in whom the Windigo spirit has actually become lodged and taken possession of the body, made manifest by a heart of ice. Furthermore, curative efforts consist largely of conjuring techniques designed to dislodge the spirit. This necessarily involves the intervention of a guardian spirit often taking the form of a totem, which will act on behalf of the conjurer. The individual who becomes a Windigo is usually convinced he has been possessed. He believes he has lost permanent control over his own actions and the only possible solution is death. He will plead for his own destruction and make no objection for his execution. **(beat)** But not always. At times, his actions prove very much the contrary. **(Short pause, he reflects and turns towards Lily and takes her hand.)**

LILY

When I was a little girl, ma and I went out in the bush one warm August day to pick blueberries. I was sitting in a patch eating the sweet fruit to my heart's content when I noticed a little bear cub not far away. I toddled over to play with it. Of course I didn't realize the danger. And ma didn't notice, being too busy picking berries. In almost an instant, the female bear was rushing towards me. A few feet away, it bounded to a halt. She must have realized that I was too small to do her baby any harm, sensed I too was a baby. My own mother was frozen with fear. She didn't move. She didn't call. She just stood there. After a minute or so, the mother bear called to her little one and they scurried off into the woods, and I began to cry. It was then that my mother came and took me away in case the mother bear returned. But there really was no need. The bear had charged because she was protecting her child. I was no threat and therefore had been left untouched. But had I meant harm, had I been a predator, she would have done everything in her power to protect her baby.

EVELYN

(Pensively) Some things just can't be explained... let me put it this way... let's say you been sittin' on a street corner smellin' piss an puke, cause all you been doin' is drinkin' whatever you can get your hands on for years to forget an try to bury all that's happened to ya... an' one day you go to take your sticky little spot but you can't. Something's happened, an' that part of your life, if you wanna call it life, is over... who knows what happens? Maybe ya see a bird in a tree, or some grass between the cracks of the street, that tell ya something, not in words... ya see, how do ya explain it? Lots of carryings-on we knew about. Take ol' Cigarette Annie, called her that cause she always had a cigarette drooping, kinda like this. **(She takes out a cigarette and droops from the corner of her lip. Removes the cigarette before continuing.)** She knew some powerful medicines that one... could suck the poison right outta ya. If ya had a complaint, she was the one ya went to. Take the time my toes started burnin'. Oh, I could hardly walk. Ol' Annie said some healin prayers an' then got right down on her knees an started suckin' my big toes. **(Confidentially)** Course I washed em first. **(beat)** Then after a while, she spit out all this green stuff into a hanky, put a pincha tobacco on the hanky an burnt it, and low an behold my feet never bothered me no more. That's the way it works some time, ya just gotta believe an **(with a wave of her hand)** forget about explainin'. **(Evelyn remains where she is, at home. She takes the cigarette in her hand and breaks it up and holds the tobacco for a second in her left hand and prays silently before putting it into the stove.)**

***

Let Me Outta Here

> This Drama piece was written and performed by Krystal Cook at the opening night of the "To Remain At A Distance Art Show" at the A Space Gallery in Victoria, B.C. on July 6, 2001.

Blackout. Audio playing of Ravens beaks pecking for 10 seconds. Voice over begins.
VILLAGE VOICE: (Voice over from behind oversized entrance door). LET ME OUTTA HERE! Piles and piles of rotting raven beaks peck at concrete. Cutting and cawing to get inside the earth. Moving in ssssllllllooooooooowwww sticky motions taunting and teasing pointy british voices to speak in tongues. Blood dialects of massacre keep me AwAy. The hidden holocaust haunts my belly. I pierce a tear for all the unloved children of the brutal rape of spirit. I sacrifice my flesh to the Salmon Belly King for the rhythm of *Kwak'wala* to belt in my bones again. Red Spots Up. Enter.

WILD WOMAN:
Costume: Mask/red and black negligee/bare feet/pregnant belly/
She lurks and movements from the depths of *Tsamus*. Seeking refuge among the souls of marching cedars. Chewing and gnawing at the moist muddy roots. Cultivating her teeth into shiny abalone weapons of war. Burping and moaning with satisfaction at the rise of brown body memory transforming into scent. She scowers the poisonous air for lost children floating in nightmares they can't wake up from. She straddles her smoldering, hairy legs around the parliament buildings and haunts them with the lusty power of her red high heels. She recreates herself in orange paint, and rituals herself to shape shift into dragonfly brilliance with the slickness of her green light. Exit. Change. *Macho Man* Music Interlude. Enter. Purple Spots Up.

TRICKSTER:
Costume: Mask/Brown leather jacket/Silver Grass skirt/Black Boots/ Gangster Hat/
My balls are soooooooooo HUGE. I can't get close to anyone. They are always in the way. Banging and busting blood around. Protecting the women and children from invisible demons that desire to devour.

Suave, sexy men glide in macho vibrations all around me and slide slickness around the people with bural cream and *Gleena*. They dance a hypnotic trance of mutilated manhood and ancient beauty (repeat last line 4 xs). Exit. Change. *I'm Too Sexy* Music Interlude. Enter. Blue Spots Up.

TRIBAL FUNK MAMA
Costume: Mask/Blue Wig/Sarong/Bare feet/Black Fur Jacket/
Tribal Funk Mama on the creative tip here with the soul vibrations from Village Voice. Yea, that sound, that sound, that SOUND the Salmon make when they are stalking me with their beauty and lusciousness. That deep murmuring of song that transports me back to the ocean depths. Where the seahorse's strip tease their magic all over the ocean floor and orca chants serenade loved ones back to the sea world. Back home to sensual shimmering mermaid royalty that rock the underworld into seaweed funk. I feel my soul filling up with salt, the raw, thick, course kind flaking from the ocean scalp into my blood injecting my memory with where my ancestors fished. I feel *Kwakwaka'wakw* rhythms stroking my bones to movement this Island, to rip it open, and let it transform, shape shift and transcend its glory and richness into sultry memories of original dream. Tribal Funk Mama here orating Village Voice into deep jazzy state of unbreakable DNA umbilical cord to LOVE. Halakasla. Exit. Blackout.

Kwak'wala word meaning place of many churches which Victoria, B.C. has become known as to many *Kwakwaka'wakw* people.

Kwak'wala word for Ooligan oil.

Section 6

Images

Lee Claremont

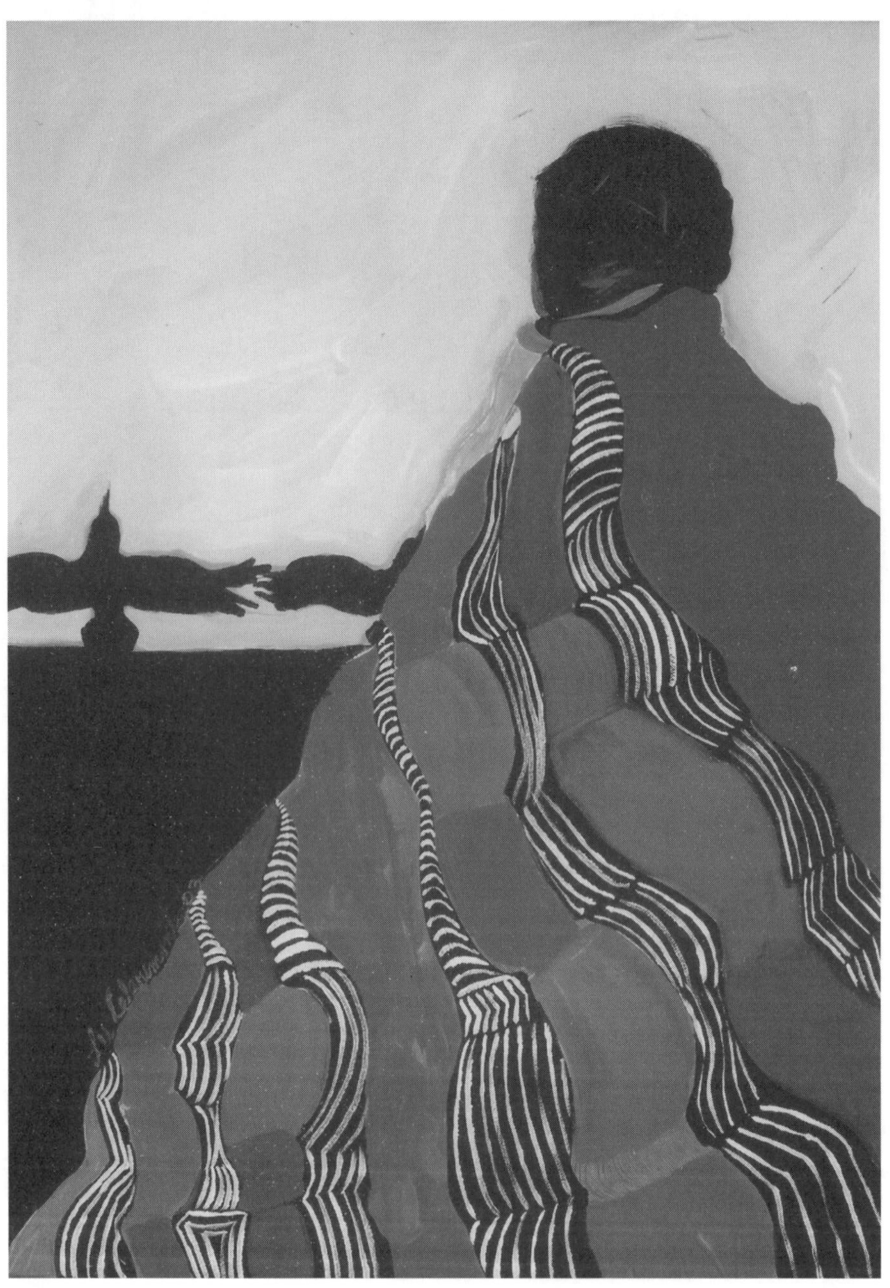

Raven Magic

Celebration

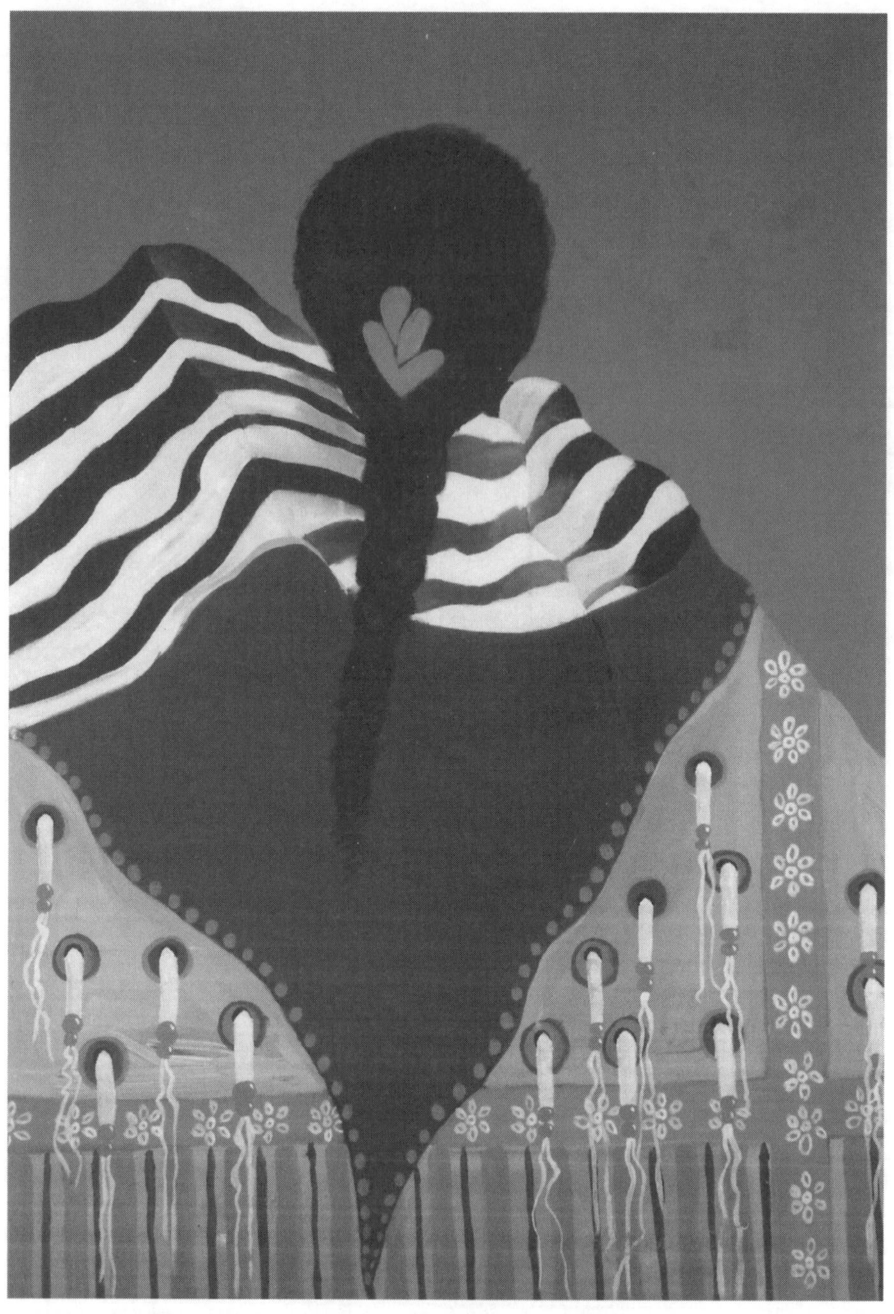

Fancy Dancer

Coming Out to Play at Midnight

Margaret Orr

Walk into Life
(Acrylic)

Walk into Life #4
(copper plate print)

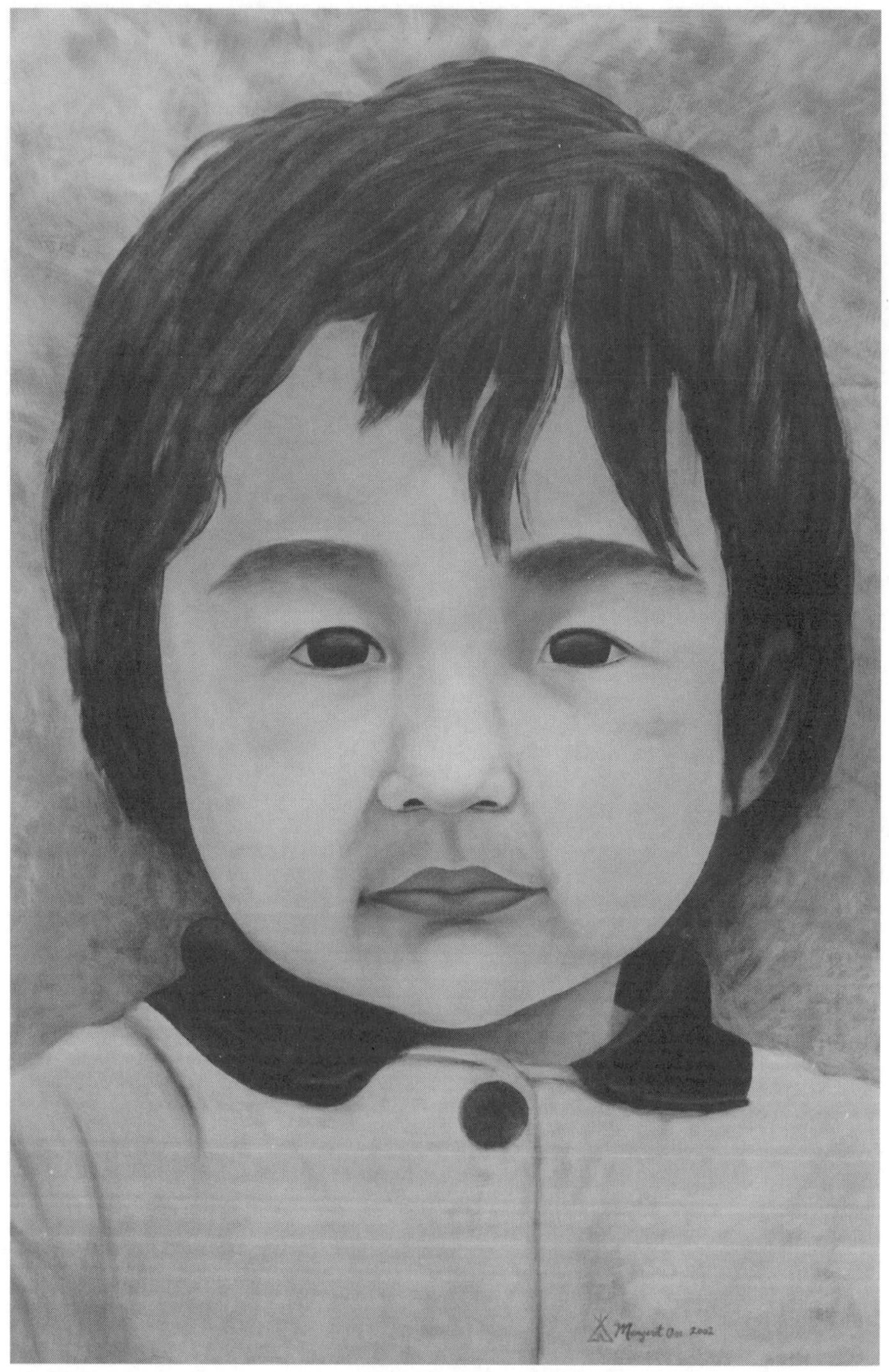

Shaenshe

Grass Dancer

Woman Sitting

Mother and Baby

A Walk in My Moccasins

Untitled

Barbara Helen Hill

Sharron Proulx

Graham Scott Proulx

Wil George

Jennifer Petahtegoose

Joy Kogawa

Jeannette Armstrong

Dawn Russel

Dennis Saddleman

Richard Van Camp

Gerry William

Leanne Flett Kruger

Drew Hayden Taylor

Tracey Jack

Karen Olson

Gordon Bird

Krystal Cook

ShoShona Kish

Robyn Kruger

Nimkish O'Sullivan Young Ing was one of the first En'owkin babies born in 1993. Born to Greg Young-Ing and Gunargie O'Sullivan.

Ashala, Sherida, Willie, Emma-Jane and Mary Rose

Mary-Rose, Emma-Jane and Willie Cohen are the children of Bill Cohen and Sherida Crane. They are also sibling to Kwanita and Tally, as well as big sister Ashala.

Sky
Parents, En'owkin Students:
ShoShona Kish
and Rene Petal/Sandy.

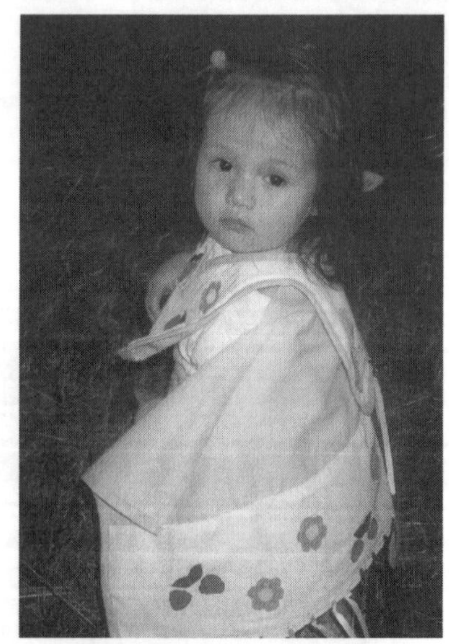

Hannah Mnookmi
daughter of Jennifer
Petahtegoose.

Kwasun is the son of Krystal Cook and Harvey Thomas.

Haley Tina Regan
Born; January 23/97
To Dawn Russell and Ron Regan.

Sage was born to Leanne Flett Kruger and John Kruger.

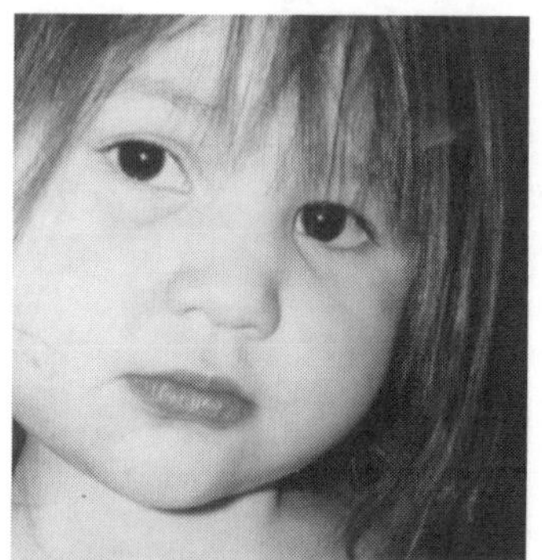

Autumn Rain was born to Leanne Flett Kruger and John Kruger.

Storm and Grace are the children of Vera Wabegijig and Larry Nicholas

Section 6

Biographies

Jeannette Christine Armstrong, Director of the En'owkin Centre and a member of the Okanagan Nation, Jeannette is a recognized Canadian author, artist and an advocate of Indigenous Peoples rights. One of her two chilren's books won the Children's Book Centre "Our Choice" award. She has published a critically acclaimed novel *Slash*, *Whispering In Shadows*, a collection of poetry *Breath Tracks* and collaborated with Douglas Cardinal on the book *Native Creative Process*. Jeannette co-edited the book *Native Poetry in Canada: A Contemporary Anthology* as well as edited *Looking at the Words of our People: First Nations Analysis of Literature*. She has published fiction, poetry and articles in a wide variety of journals and anthologies. She has a BFA, First Class, from the University of Victoria. Jeannette was recently distinguished with an Honourary Doctorate of Letters from St. Thomas University, Fredericton.

Suzi Bekkattla is from St George's Hill, Saskatchewan and now lives in Vancouver BC. She is proud to be fluent in the Dene language. Leaving En'owkin Center in 1999, and completing a third year of a Bachelors of Education at the University of Saskatchewan, Suzi journeyed to Hong Kong to teach ESL. Upon returning to Canada, she attended the Aboriginal Film School at the Native Education Center. She has worked at Young Eagles Healing Lodge youth Treatment Center in Vancouver and has volunteered at Potters Place Mission Center. Currently Suzi works as a First Nations Support worker for the Vancouver School Board. Her dreams are to open a library in Northern Saskatchewan, interview elders and utilize their knowledge to write, and to make films.

Gordon Bird is from Lac La Ronge, Saskatchewan. Born August 13, 1967, he has a Cree and French background. A recovering alcoholic and drug addict, April 11, 2004 will be nine years of sobriety for Gordon. His Spirit name is Circle Dancing Eagle. He has had his poetry published and played the lead role in the play Elvis Goodrunner. He has worked as a lighting technician for theaters. He has a deep appreciation for music, art and all artistic genre's. He loves to write drama and has a dream to one day become a film director. "I learn a lot from being out on the land. There are many valuable lessons that come from the land about how to live upon Mother Earth."

Trevor Cameron is Métis. He is an independant filmmaker and writer. He has a certificate of recomendation in film making from the Vancouver Film School.

Lee Claremont was born in Woodstock, Ontario of Mohawk and Irish ancestry. She is a member of the Six Nations in Oshweken, Ontario. Lee now resides in Kelowna, BC. She is well known for her vibrant paintings. Her work can be found in collections in Europe, the Orient and North America. Lee keeps busy teaching art at the En'owkin Center, as well as being a professsional artist and enjoying her three daughters and six grandchildren.

Crystal Lee Clark is from Fort McMurray, Alberta. She has recently completed an Education degree from the University of British Columbia with support from the Métis Nation of Vancouver. Crystal has a Bachelor of Fine Arts Degree from the University of Victoria, and has also completed a New Media Degree from Vancouver Film School with a scholarship from the BC Festival of the Arts. Crystal is also a graduate of the En'owkin's Creative Writing and Fine Arts program. While in Vancouver, she worked with a team of youth to create a public art site based on sustainability practices of the past and present to build a healthy future (www.collective-echoes.org). She is now teaching and plans to continue writing and creating visual art.

Brent Peacock-Cohen is an Okanagan poet currently completing his Ph D at Ohio State University. His poetry attempts to connect intellectualism, tradition and self-determination. Brent is a former En'owkin instructor who taught in the Indigenous Political Development and Leadership program. He hopes his life's journey brings him back to the En'owkin Centre.

Krystal Cook is a Kwakwaka'wakw Woman from the Namgis First Nation of Alert Bay, BC. She is a graduate of the En'owkin International School of Writing (UVIC) and the Centre for Indigenous Theatres' Native Theatre School Program. She is a performance artist, poet, facilitator of Healing through the Arts and the mother to two sons, Kwasun and Rayn.

Sherida Crane is a Blackfoot/mixed blood writer of the Siksika Nation in Alberta. She graduated from the En'owkin in 1997 where she received the William Armstrong Scholarship for Poetry and the Simon Lucas Jr. Memorial Scholarship. Her play "Shifting Savage Moods" was workshopped in Calgary. She is currently working on a collection of poetry and short stories. Her poetry and stories reflects personal spiritual struggles and healing. Sherida and her amazing children, Ashala 14, Mary-Rose 6, Emma 4, and baby Willy 1 1/2 reside in the Similkameen Valley, BC.

Barb Fraser is a Cree woman from northern Saskatchewan. The eldest of eight, she spent her childhood playing with the past in a museum owned by parents John and Mathilda. Barb is a blues singer who graduated from En'owkin in 1992 then travelled to Germany and Switzerland. She was published in literary and environmental journals and produced a radio show. Barb completed a BA in Botany and Native Studies and received a certificate in Environmental Education. Currently, she is a Manager at the Sciences Program with the Federation of Saskatchewan Indian Nations where she promotes the art of Traditional Science. Future plans include a Masters degree, a one-woman show, a blues CD and to lead a happy life after forty.

Wil George is from the Tsleil Wauth Nation (Burrard Indian Band). He studies Writing and English Literature at UVIC. Wil has been published in various anthologies such as *Gatherings: En'owkin Journal of First North American Peoples* and *Mocambo Nights.*

Barbara 'Helen' Hill is a writer and visual artist from Six Nations of the Grand River Territory in Southern Ontario, Canada. She is a Cayuga/Mohawk woman, mother of three and grandmother of two beautiful granddaughters. After graduating with an MA in American Studies, Helen changed careers due to ill health and started to focus more on her artwork. Helen is the author of *Shaking the Rattle: Healing the Trauma of Colonization*, now in its second edition, and has stories and poems published in various anthologies. She is the owner/operator of Shadyhat Books, Publishing and Art Company. Helen has ventured into fibre and textile art as a new medium.

William Horne is a member of the Sannich Indian Band. He is an artist who attended the Foundations in Indigenous Fine Arts Program at the En'owkin Centre.

Tracey Jack is an award winning broadcast journalist and producer for television news and documentaries. She is a member of the Okanagan Nation, born and raised on the Penticton Indian Band. Currently she is the Program Director for the Indigenous Arts Service Organization. Mrs.Jack has been published in Raven's Eye (AMMSA) and Aboriginal Voices. Her current works include producing segments for the CHBC-Television program "Okanagan Now." Mrs. Jack was awarded First and Second place for the documentaries "Crying in the Dark" and "REZcovery" at the 2003 International Native American Journalists Association conference. Mrs. Jack has been granted the Award of Excellence as a finalist for the British Columbia Association of Broadcasters and the Canadian Association of Broadcasters Award. She has recently been granted a Bell Media/APTN scholarship from Ryerson Polytech to establish programming with CBC Radio on a freelance basis. Her lifelong passion is to balance stories from an Aboriginal perspective that creates dialogue to dispel ignorance and racism.

ShoShona Kish is an Anishinabekwe singer / song writer and spoken word artist from Toronto, Canada. Her powerful earthy voice and diverse musical style are influenced by her First Nations roots as well as soul, folk, blues and jazz. Her songs speak about the beauty and complexity of her people and of the landscape we all share as part of this creation. She has hosted and performed in festivals and conferences across North America, traveled to Hawaii and throughout Canada to lend her voice to several CD recordings. She studied music at Carleton University and Creative Writing at the En'owkin International School of Writing in British Columbia. Currently, she is working on her first solo CD project with the support of the Canada Council for the Arts and a collaborative project fusing the talents of international Indigenous artists to create a unique new sound.

Robyn Kruger is an Interdisciplinary Arts Performer. She works with contemporary mythical design concepts and her work reflects and is influenced by her First Nation Okanagan heritage. She has a certificate in Indigenous Fine Arts from the En'owkin Centre and plans to continue her education at the University of Victoria

Maurice Kenny is a Mohawk born in Watertown, NY, in 1929. He was educated at Butler University, St. Lawrence University and New York University. Maurice has been the co-editor of the literary review magazine *Contact/II*, editor/publisher of Strawberry Press and poetry editor of *Adirondac Magazine*, Poet-in-Residence at North Country Community College and visiting professor at the University of Oklahoma, and the En'owkin Centre in Canada. Maurice's work has been published in journals, including *American Indian Quarterly, Blue Cloud Quarterly* and *The New York Time*s. In 2000, Maurice received the Elder Recognition Award from the Wordcraft Circle of Native Writers. His book of poems, *Blackrobe: Isaac Jogues, B. March 11, 1607, D. October 18, 1646* was nominated for the Pulitzer Prize. Maurice is the recipient of a National Public Radio Award for Broadcasting. His book *The Mama Poems* received the American Book Award in 1984.

Joy Kogawa is the author of the critically acclaimed novel *Obasan*. Her most recent works are a novel, *The Rain Ascends* by Penguin and a selection of poems, *A Garden of Anchors* by Mosaic; both published in 2003. She is currently rewriting a second novel, *Itsuka*. She is active in the community currency movement, and involved with The Toronto Dollar.

Leanne Flett Kruger is Métis of the Flett family in Northern Manitoba. Leanne is a graduate of the En'owkin Centre's Creative Writing Program. She has taken courses in publishing at Simon Fraser University and works as the Production and Distribution Manager of Theytus Books Ltd. Her daughters Sage and Autumn Rain are members of the Okanagan Nation and they enjoy spending time in the En'owkin Centre's gathering space.

Joseph Thomas Wayne Kruger is an Okanagan/Shuswap living on the Penticton Indian Band Reserve. Born on October 4, 1981. The need to learn and explore new ideas and ways of thinking is the motivation for everything he does. His writing is influenced by Indigenous cultures and philosophies, Eastern Philosophies, and his own day-to-day observations. He currently attends the En'owkin Centre.

Dr. Hartmut Lutz is the Chair of American and Canadian Studies at the University of Greifswald in Germany and has been teaching Canadian literature there since 1994. He obtained a doctorate magna cum laude in English literature from Tubingen University and taught British and American Studies at Osnabruck University from 1975 to 1994. He has visited Canada on several extended research trips funded by the Canadian Government Faculty Research and Faculty Enrichment Programs. He has also researched and taught in Native Studies at the University of California Davis, the First Nations University of Canada (Regina) and Dartmouth College. The research fields studied by Dr. Lutz cover an impressive range, with particular focus on Canadian Aboriginal literature. Dr. Lutz has worked assiduously to understand and promote Canadian culture, especially an indigenous perspective on Aboriginal literatures.

Rasunah Marsden of Anishinabe and French ancestry was born in Brandon, Manitoba and obtained teacher training and post graduate degrees in Fine Arts and Design. Rasunah wrote and taught overseas in the cities Brisbane, Jakarta, Perth and Sydney. She taught at the En'owkin Centre for several years until accepting a position to coordinate the Digital Film and Television program at the Native Education Center in Vancouver where she and her four grown children reside. Rasunah is a widely anthologized Aboriginal writer with several poems featured in Native Poetry in Canada (2001). She edited *Crisp Blue Edges* (2000), a first collection of Aboriginal creative non-fiction in North America. Currently she continues as chair and webmaster of the Subud Writer's International (SWI) website.

Nikki Maier graduated from the En'owkin's writing program in 1997. "The En'owkin is an amazing place to start university!" Nikki attended the University of Victoria for third year writing studies with a full scholarship from the National Aboriginal Achievement Foundation. Nikki worked at Redwire Native Youth Media office, and later as editor of *The Long Haul*, an anti-poverty newspaper. Recently, Nikki was featured on the *Redwire Native Magazine*'s 'Our Voice is Our Weapon and Our Bullets are the Truth' CD. Nikki is Tlinglit on her mother's side and her father is from Trinidad. This year, she will be completing a Bachelor of Arts in English at Okanagan University.

Karen W. Olson is Cree/Ojibway from the Peguis First Nation in Manitoba. A former journalist with CBC Radio, she also wrote freelance articles for *Weetamah, Windspeaker* and *First Perspective*. A single parent to Krista Rose, Karen graduated from the En'owkin Centre in 1999 as a recipient of the Simon Lucas Jr. award for fiction. After graduating from the University of Victoria with a BFA, she returned to the En'owkin Centre as the creative arts instructor in 2002. Karen has published two short stories and was awarded a Canada Council grant to continue work on a novel set in the pow wow world. Karen is also writing a young adult historical novel about the 1907 illegal surrender of St. Peter's Indian Reserve.

Margaret Orr is Cree, born March 11, 1962, in Prince Albert Saskatchewan and grew up on the coastline of James Bay in Northern Quebec where her mother, Gracie Snowboy, was raised. She graduated with a fine arts degree at CEGEP in Hull, 1993 and from Saskatchewan Indian Federated College with a Bachelor of Fine Arts Degree in 1998. Margaret graduated from the En'owkin Centre's Creative Writing program in 2001 and spent one year in the Indigenous Political Development and Leadership program which she completed in 2002. Much of Margaret's knowledge stems from the land, she draws inspiration from all parts of the country she travels with her children.

Gunargie O'Sullivan is from the Kwakuilth Nation, in Alert Bay. She is a performer and the proud mother of a daughter, Nimkish. Gunargie studied at the En'owkin to explore her talents as a visual artist.

Jennifer Petahtegoose is a member of the Elk Clan of Whitefish Lake First Nation, Ojibway and British ancestry. She is a graduate of En'owkin's Fine Arts Program. She holds a Bachelor of Education and a Bachelor of Arts in Psychology and Native Studies. Presently she teaches Grade 5/6 in Sudbury and is the proud mother of Hannah Mnookmi. Jennifer is a fancy shawl dancer. Her inspiration comes from the beautiful people she has met, through the shimmer of colors inside the pow wow circle and through her dreams. Her influences as a painter include Norval Morrisseau, George Littlechild, Arthur Shilling, and Wassily Kandinsky. Jennifer had her first solo art show at the Ojibwe Cultural Foundation in Manitoulin Island in July 2002.

Brenda Prince (Middle of the Sky Woman) is Anishinabe, born and raised in Winnipeg, Manitoba. She has lived in Calgary, Victoria and Penticton and she now makes her home in Vancouver, BC. She graduated from the En'owkin School of Writing in 1996 and is now a 4th year English Major at UBC and works in the Downtown Eastside as a Researcher/Evaluator. Forty years young, she is the proud mother of Raven, Robin and Dakota, and proud grandmother to Tatiana and loves her cat Poozhas.

Graham Scott Proulx is a misplaced Métis writer, artist and educator. Hailing from the lands of the Odawa, he now resides in Sto:lo territory in the Greater Vancouver area with his cat, Raven. The En'owkin Centre forever altered his life course; the intensive creative and decolonizing experience empowered him to share the sacred gift of knowledge with generations to come. Thanks to a few friends and family members (teachers in their own right) who are able to tolerate him he has begun to sprout roots. The invaluable and continued support, inspiration and influence of his mentors and peers at En'owkin helped procure a path that he never dreamed possible to walk. K^{w}uk^{w}uk^{w}stx^{w}.

Sharron Proulx is *Nokomis* to Willow & Jessinia, and mum to Graham, Barb & Adrian. She is published in literary journals and has written two books, *Where the Rivers Join: A Personal Account of Healing from Ritual Abuse* (under a pseudonym) and *What The Auntys Say*. Both books were short listed for national awards. Meegwich to Jeannette Armstrong for her incredible talent as a writer and a mentor to so many of our youth.

Fred Roberds is a member of the N'kmapls First Nation in Vernon, BC. Fred graduated from the En'owkin Centre in 1999 with a Visual Arts certificate and in 2002 with a Creative Writing certificate. He has been painting and drawing since he was a young boy. He describes his writing style as an exploration of the darker side of human nature.

Armand Garnet Ruffo is from Northern Ontario and is a member of the Biscotasing branch of the Sagamok First Nation. his work is strongly influenced by his Anishnaabe heritage. Currently he resides in Ottawa where he teaches in the Department of English Language and Literature at Carleton University. Published works include: *At Geronimo's Grave, Grey Owl: The Mystery of Archie Belaney* and *Opening in the Sky.*

Dawn M. Russell works for the Surrey School District as an Aboriginal Support Worker, sharing her experiences as a member of the Okanagan Nation. Dawn and her daughter, Haley, are active in their community and strive to be positive role models.

Dennis Saddleman was a student of the En'owkin Centre, from 1995 to 1997. He went home to write poems and stories about himself. Dennis has published some work with First Nation's newsletters and newspapers. Several times, he was a keynote speaker at Residential School conferences. His biggest achievement was being elected as a Band Councilor at his communities Chief and Council election. Dennis often finds himself back at the En'owkin Centre to see how everyone is doing.

Lillian Sam is a graduate of the Creative Writing Program at the En'owkin Centre. She is from the Carrier Nation . She worked extensively to compile and transcribe stories from her Elders for the book, Nak'azdli Elders Speak *Nak'azdli t'enne Yahulduk.*

Lorne Joseph Simon, *1960-1994*. Born on the Big Cove Reserve in New Brunswick and raised according to Mi'kmaq traditions, Lorne was fluent in speaking and writing his language. He graduated from the En'owkin School of Writing in 1992. Lorne was the first En'owkin writing student to be published by Theytus Books. While his book was in final production Lorne was killed in a car accident on October 8, 1994. *Stones and Switches* was released after his death and has since received critical acclaim.

Drew Hayden Taylor is an award winning playwright, author, journalist, film maker and lecturer. During the last two decades, over fifty-five productions of Drew's plays have been shown in Canada, the United States and Europe. In film and video, Drew has directed three documentaries including the very popular National Film Board production, *Redskins Tricksters and Puppy Stew*, an examination of Native humour. Several of his thirteen books including *Funny You Don't Look Like One* and *Toronto at Dreamer's Rock*, are in multiple printings and are used in school curriculum across Canada. Drew is an Ojibway from Ontario's Curve Lake First Nations in central Ontario.

Richard Van Camp was born and raised in Fort Smith, NWT, and is a member of the Dogrib Nation. He is the author of *The Lesser Blessed*, *Angel Wing Splash Pattern* and two children's books *A Man Called Raven* and *What's the Most Beautiful Thing You Know About Horses?*

Vera Wabegijig is a twenty-nine year old Scorpio Anishnawbe writer, videographer, and mother of two most beautiful girls, Storm and Grace. She lives in Vancouver, BC and loves the words, rhythms and beats that naturally occur and surround her – this is where her inspiration comes from.

Jacqueline Wachell is a Métis artist and mother of three. She was a student of the En'owkin Centre NAPAT program. She works in many artistic disciplines and had her work featured at the 2003 Splitting the Sky Arts Festival.

The En'owkin Centre
Indigenous School of Writing and Arts

The En'owkin Indigenous Fine Arts and Writing Program is a one year credit program leading to a Foundations in Indigenous Fine Arts Certificate, jointly awarded by the En'owkin Centre and the University of Victoria. Established Aboriginal writers, dramatists and visual artists work directly with the students to explore their own unique voice, thereby promoting understanding of the beauty and complexity of Aboriginal Peoples. Courses focus on techniques and forms of creative expression in Poetry, Fiction, Drama, Creative Non-fiction and Visual Arts.

For a full calendar and registration information contact:

Registrar
En'owkin Centre
Lot 45, Green Mountain Road.
RR #2, Site 50, Comp.8
Penticton, BC
V2A-6J7
Phone: (250) 493-7181
Fax (250) 493-5302
email: enowkin@vip.net
www.enowkincentre.ca